TWIST

A WHY CHOOSE DARK TABOO ROMANCE

LAYLA MOON

Twisted Friction

Copyright © 2024 by Layla Moon

The story, all names, characters, and incidents portrayed in this production are fictitious. No identification with actual persons (living or deceased), places, buildings, and products is intended or should be inferred. However, the author would like to admit here that this book is **inspired** by both her past experiences and deranged imagination.

This book is based in Australia and is therefore written in UK English

DISCLOSURE: I have been having consistent issues with the formatting program Atticus—it has been deleting words, and already since publishing I have noticed even after saving the file there have been <u>more</u> deleted words or even swapping words around. Please understand I am trying to correct this and is also out of my control as it seems to be happening even as I am in the program fixing errors. I am doing my best to make sure I have this book the best it can be, but technical errors are preventing me from doing so.

Book Cover by Layla Moon

Illustrations by Layla Moon

Edited by Brittany at BLD Editing

TWISTED FRICTION

A DARK TABOO ROMANCE

LAYLA MOON

BOOKS BY LAYLA MOON

The Offering – A Dark Thriller Romance — #1 Bestselling
Erotic Thriller
Twisted Friction – A Dark Taboo Romance
Twisted Friction – *Explicit Edition*

BOOKS COMING SOON

After The Rain – A Dark Suspense Romance
(sequel to The Offering)
Title to be Announced – A Dark Stalker Romance
Title to be Announced – A Dark Taboo Stalker Romance
Title to be Announced – A Dark Psychological Erotic
Romance
and more...

To stay up to date with book signings, new releases, behind the
scenes and giveaways visit **www.laylamoonauthor.com**
Also consider signing up to Layla's exclusive newsletter here

This book contains explicit adult content. Inside you will see a shit tonne of profanity, a lot of fucking sex, sex with random people both forced and not forced, hate fucking, revenge, banter, and some really questionable scenes.

<u>You will question your morals.</u>

And I will laugh while watching you do so.

This book isn't a love story by any means, but everyone deserves a happy ending, which I promise they do get. Even if they're siblings. And yes, there is an ending, and that is exactly that—an ending.

There is no sequel, there is no reunion. It is simply **<u>The End.</u>**

This book was intended to be a pallet cleanser from my debut novel *The Offering.*

The content warnings for **this** book are here should you wish to read them. #becauseyourmentalhealthmatters and yadayada.

If you prefer to go in dry, don't say I didn't warn you!

Because *everything* in this book is all kinds of fucked up!

I love you, I appreciate you, so please enjoy

PLAYLIST

Pretty Boy – *Isabel Larosa (unreleased at time of publish but you can find it on TikTok)*

Sugar – *Sleep Token*

Sephiroth – *PierceTheSkies*

Sick Like Me – *In This Moment*

NASTY – *Russ*

my strange addiction – *Billie Eilish*

No Mercy – *Austin Giorgio*

Living Hell – *Bella Poarch*

trigger warning – *Christian French*

Surround Sound – *JID, 21 Savage, Baby Tate*

You Know I'm No Good – *Amy Winehouse*

KILL4ME – *Marilyn Manson*

and more...
Scan to add Spotify playlist...

"I had *no* idea I had that kink"

- you, a few moments from now

PART ONE
Twister

Have you ever fucked in front of someone before? If you said yes, congratulations—you're a whore. Hey, me too, sis.

Me-fucking-too.

I guess we find our kinks one way or another. Don't mock it until you try it, right? Or whatever it is normal people say. I guess, what I'm trying to say is, you *need* to try it. Or don't. I don't give a fuck. But if you do, can I watch?

Or better yet...can you watch me?

Shit, I'd even teach you—or make you, the choice is yours, really. Though it's not really a choice then, is it? Look, because I feel like being nice today, here's a little something about me that you should know: I love games. Playthings—*fucktoys*. Cock, pussy, pool balls, car shifters, handbrakes. Whatever you have to offer.

I'll take any*thing* and any*one*.

So, I guess my last question is...are you ready to play with me?

PART TWO
Drip

Uh, YOU FORGOT ONE important little detail, *sis.*

There are rules to our little game...and there is nothing I hate more *than disobedience.*

ONE
Twister

FUCKING HELL, THE ADRENALINE. That orgasmic rush of fire-like electricity shock waving through my veins, like a cylinder of NOS pumping through me. *Eyes on me.* My fucking favourite thing—other than drifting, of course.

I was fighting for each breath, begging for more but instinctively trying to hold myself together to last longer. I had my back stretched over the arch of the fuel tank of the blacked-out Kawasaki ZX6R, and looked down at my ankles that were propped over the shoulders of my new plaything—the guy who had just lost the race against Drip.

His head shoved between my thighs.

And his mouth sealed over my pussy. *Such a hungry little thing.*

I banded a tuft of his curly hair between my fingers and tugged his head to the left, guiding his tongue as it rolled tight, precise swirls over my clit. I moaned and shuddered from the static vibrations of his talented mouth. He groaned in response, pressing his weight into my waist with his thumbs.

He was nervous. I could feel it in the heat that was radiating from his hands on my skin while his tongue worked my pussy. But with each lick and suck, he lost himself more and more. *Fuck—this is too good.* I was on the brink of coming undone. *Hold it in, hold it in.* Almost the best head I had gotten to date, but I dared not tell that to Drip, who I caught sight of in the corner of my eye. But he was gone again as I rolled my head back from pleasure. *Eyes on me, I fucking love it.*

His sharp grey eyes pinned on me, and his chest was working hard for every breath, which only made me fight even harder for each of mine. He was leaning back against his bike with his arms crossed *in that way*—the way a hot, possessive boyfriend does when he's watching another man eat out his girl.

At his command.

With a raging fucking boner.

So fucking hard.

He had on one of my favourite singlets of his. The white torn fabric hung loosely, yet taut in the right places over his corded muscles. The spaghetti straps barely held his chest in, and in turn, showed each carefully articulated tattoo that bled through the hue of his skin. I'd known him for so long without an inch of blank canvas other than his face, I didn't even remember what he looked like when we were kids.

A moan broke through my lips and Drip's fists clenched. He drew in a chest full of air and shifted his hips. *Fuck, I want to taste his pre cum right now, but not yet.* He could wait. God, it was getting harder to focus on two things at once. My orgasm was building quickly.

I loved the way he looked at me when someone was going to make me cum, and I loved watching him watch me. But dammit to fucking hell, this guy was good. I couldn't concentrate.

I shuddered out another moan, arching my chest to the warm, dark night sky. My crop tee rode up as I stretched back, unveiling my bare tits. The guy's hand reached up and tightened over one, squeezing hard and slowly finding my nipple. I squirmed as the sensation from the pads of his finger lit my skin on fire. Panting hard, my orgasm built as he traced the sensitive skin of my areola before trailing his touch over the piercing lodged in my nipple. I yelped in pure heaven as he pinched my now-tightened nipple between his fingers, then released and caressed the area.

I rolled my hips to meet more of his tongue. *I need to cum. But just...a little longer.*

"Good boy. She likes what you're doing," Drip purred, praising the kid. His tone almost cracked, it was so low and husky. It usually dropped that low when he was extremely turned on, roaring right under your skin.

As if encouragement was all the guy needed, I felt a hot breath seep from his grin, and then a set of teeth nip slightly at the vertical metal bar that impaled my clit.

"Ah, fuck," I cried. *Make me bleed.*

I lifted my ass up, edging him on to bite it. He paused, hovering with the two balls behind his teeth. "Do it," I begged, my teeth clenched shut, my climax on the tip of his touch. He closed his grip over my clit, the bar straining against my skin and nicking it slightly. Everything skyrocketed in my brain like a fucking field of fireworks were going off, and I rolled into an intense climax. He groaned and breathed heavily against my skin, intensifying my orgasm. "Oh, fuck," I pleaded mindlessly for something to fill me.

"Pretty boy," Drip tsked before continuing, "there's something you should know about my sister. She likes pain. Keep it up, and the time I allow you with her won't last as long as you want."

That was true, and I *hated* that it was. I was really enjoying this one; he was different. But it was the norm for us.

These losers paid big money...for *me*. Once a month, we ran a big race. I take any*one and* any*thing* with four wheels, and my brother takes those on two. If they won, they got *me*.

Permanently.

And everything that comes with me. A title, for the most part. And millions of dollars. Every estate we own. Every car. Every bike. *And Drip's city.* The Underground. But if we won...I got to do whatever the fuck I wanted with them. I got to decide. We could simply just take their money and go, like normal human beings. But I was not a normal human being.

I was born corrupted. A default. I was non refundable.

Only disposable.

Drugs used to be the only thing that made me feel...*something*. Until I found another unhealthy habit,—which only got me into the mess I was in now—*hiding that secret from my brother.* And then I found yet another fucking problem, just to replace the other defect of mine.

Sex.

And a whole lot of it.

But there was an itch that hounded me.

An itch that needed scratching, intensifying with each passing day.

I had a problem. I knew that. But sex wasn't a crime. Killing someone was. *If only my brother knew how good it feels,—how good it could be if we did both of those things...together.*

After a while, auctioning me off eventually got boring, because no one ever won. But then we started telling them that we were brother and sister, and the rewards got even better. I enjoyed seeing their faces drop to their asses, but I think Drip frothed over it more than I did. That shit got him hard. Real hard.

I tried pulling myself back to the moment and the guy between my legs peered up at me from under his lashes. He moved back enough so that he could catch a breath and wipe his now-crimson mouth with his tongue, his face evincing the relish of my metallic flavours.

I furrowed my brows. I didn't usually notice the features of my fuck toys so well, but for some reason, *his* stood out. Vibrant, energising olive green eyes. And freckles, jeez. And his eyes were full of lust and hunger. *Fuck, he is too cute and innocent. What in the fuck is he doing, getting himself involved in this lifestyle?* And he was terrible at riding a bike. Drip shouldn't have let him race. *So why did he?*

He lowered his head again, not taking his eyes from mine, his tongue finding my clit once more. My climax didn't even need working again, it was already close. So close. But he slowed again. I didn't want it to end, but I knew it would once Drip had enough of him. *Can't we just...keep him?*

TWO

Twister

"Ah—ahhh. FUCK," I cried out. I rolled my head back, losing myself in the pleasure. He maintained this pace, building me up and letting me go again until I was physically incapable of using the pink noodles in my head that scientists apparently call a fucking brain. It was basically fucking soup, at that point.

Loving the pain and pleasure, but wanting another release, he gave me a wink and then became nothing but a blur. I felt the heat of his grin again, and the night air cooled my flesh, making me shiver. He tittered. He was liking it...turning me into jelly.

In front of my *brother*.

Who he knew about.

And was not *at all* bothered by it.

It wasn't often that we found one of *us*. One who's into what we're into. But this kid didn't seem the slightest bit phased by it...by us. The others always were. In fact, he was quite the opposite. He had lit up like the Australian sun when Drip had mentioned that I was his sister. All the guy could mutter out was a mindless, breathless, *'Fuck.'*

Through my mind fuzz, I heard Drip mirror him and chuckle.

"I think we just found our new playtoy, Twister," he groaned, tugging at his jeans. He just *had* to make more room for the throbbing chaos that was pounding underneath them. *Fuck, he is...god, I can't even deal with this man.* Warmth swirled my belly at the thought of the two of them taking turns with me, like pass the parcel. But Drip was more of a watcher.

Heat started to fill me. Fingers, long fingers. *Oh, fuck.* He curled them upward, shifting the weight of his hand to my ass and pushing the tips to the knot in my belly that was suddenly on fire, completely unfolding my orgasm. The sounds of erotic pleasure from my painfully built climax coiled harder than the last, shredding through the air like tearing fabric. The hot liquid from my pussy rapidly flowed into his mouth. Whatever he couldn't catch trickled down my ass crack and onto the leather underneath me.

By the time I could focus my vision again, Drip was standing by the kid's shoulder, back by at least two feet, both of them hungrily hovering their gazes on the mess on the bike's seat. I propped myself onto my elbows with a grin, proud of the juices that sparkled underneath me.

As I caught my breath, I took a very long look at the man who just made me squirt on his bike. Sweat dripped down his forehead over his youthful face, a flushed complexion over his cheeks. Velvet stained his chin and down his neck, trailing under the tee that was ironically covered in the band members of the *Gorillaz*. Only one of my favourite bands from my teenage years. Floating my eyes further down, I saw his tight muscles. He was lean and had a very fit physique and...had a very endowed bulge. And a wet patch.

"Now, do we clean up her mess, or add to it, hmm?" Drip toyed. He dragged out his words like a demand.

"You would let me do that, too?" the young one asked nervously.

"I own that pussy, kid. I can do whatever the fuck I want with it," Drip declared. The metal of his tongue bar clattered over his teeth as he rolled his tongue over his lips and then toyed with his tooth. The look on the kid's face turned wide-eyed. *Is he...a virgin?*

I smiled. *Oh, this is just too good.* I tucked my legs up, planting my feet on the back seat. Slowly, I spread them open, then closed them again and swayed them from side to side invitingly. I sighed in that way that made them both purse their lips. They watched as I shifted my hand down my body, splitting my fold and finding myself, neither making the move to help. *Come on, don't just stand there. Somebody fuck me, dammit.*

18

My fluid twinkled under the streetlights of the city, right beside the river. Drip had his crew close the road off for the race, like always. I swiped a section of the fluid and inserted two fingers into my swollen hole, both of them shifting their hips as I finger fucked myself.

"Ware you from, *pretty boy?*"

"Uh, Malta?" he replied nervously, almost in question.

"So you're hung, then?"

I moaned, my tits rising and falling to my breath. He panted but held himself—just. "F-fuck," he quivered, taking a quick glance at Drip, waiting for his next cue.

"Yes, okay, let's do that. Pull your pants down, pretty boy," Drip commanded, and he did exactly that. I gnawed on my bottom lip when his impressive erection bounced free.

*Un*holy-fucking-shit. *Yes, case closed.* "Oh," I whimpered. It was as fucking perfectly thick as it was long, portioned just right. And now that I was swollen, I would have a very hard time fitting that in. *Even fucking better.*

"Good boy," Drip tapped the passenger seat of the bike. The air fanning my pussy sent a shiver through my body. "Now, sit here." He did as he was instructed, and I shifted back so he had just enough room.

I was face to face with the sweet sucker who lost the race, losing his bike that we both sat on and his cash as a result. But all of those things were clearly the furthest in his mind. His eyes were like glass; I could see every word and thought run across them. Despite the pussy sitting inches from his cock, he wasn't there for me. Or for the city. That much was clear. He wanted in. Why, was anyone's guess. I guess Drip saw something in him that I couldn't.

"Yes...you're *our* little toy now, kid," Drip toyed.

I lifted my legs up behind my new plaything, leaning forward so my nipple piercings pressed lightly over his skin and my hot breath made him shiver.

"Oh, we're keeping him?"

"I think you know the answer to that, sis."

He gulped and his cock throbbed, the wet tip making contact with my clit. "What is your name?" I teased, letting his tip press lightly at my entrance.

"Uh, M-M-" he whimpered, unable to finish the sentence. "Are you a virgin?" I asked, putting my hand over my boob and toying with it.

"Fuck. Uhm. Y-yes."

A breathy moan hammered from within me. *Even fucking better, and just as I expected.*

"Tell me your name," I pressed. I wanted to know whose virginity I was taking.

"Mitch."

"Mitch," I repeated in a breath.

"Now, pretty boy...Mitch. I want you to grab that gorgeous looking cock of yours and load it into my sister's fine little pussy," Drip growled in his ear.

"But I—" Drip cut him off, slapping his palms over his shoulders, making him jump. Drip looked furious, only for a second. He rapidly drew in a breath through his nose, closing his eyes to pull himself back again.

"This is my city, kid. You'll learn quickly. If you want in, you gotta earn it. Do what I fucking tell you, *when* I tell you. Say no again, and you'll have another thing coming," Drip threatened, then he changed his tone entirely. "So, when I ask you to fuck my sister until she can't remember her own name, and she can only scream mine...then you'll earn my respect."

"Who *are* you people?" Mitch muttered, shaking his head with a glint in his eyes. But the edge in his voice sounded relieved, like he had just found comfort.

I gave Drip one final look, turning my smile to the side and waiting for his final tick of approval. But being the sassy bitch I was, I *didn't* fucking listen. I loved pissing him off.

So, I jolted my hips forward with everything I had, letting *all* of Mitch penetrate my pussy.

THREE
Drip

Twister was made for this shit. She was your hot, filthy, horny poster girl who fed off being watched. A submissive little thing, but fuck around and she could rip your balls from the sac before you could say, *"Oh, shit."*

Seeing her fuck someone on a motorbike had sent me into some kind of wicked fucking overdrive. He'd had one hand cupped on her boob, while the other circled her clit, osculating her tight little body forwards and backwards over his meaty cock. I was losing my fucking mind.

Her other tit bounced with her rhythm, her pace fastening and slowing. She had a good handful, and they put up a good bounce when you fucked her good and hard. She had a tattoo under her boobs, running down to her belly button. A flower of some kind, with what looked like a spiderweb behind it. We used to play little games when we first started fucking. How much cum could I manage to get in the lines?

Twister was…something else.

Elite. Everything was in the right places.

She was my little fuck toy. One that would break if you gave it to her hard enough, but she always managed to take it. Fixed her attitude, half the time. But the rest of her was a loose fucking screw.

As much as she annoyed the piss out of me, I loved her. It was *us* against the world. I had lost my brother. I wasn't going to lose her too.

I undid the button of my chinos and pulled out my cock, which had been nagging me to stroke it for far too long. The cheeky fucking bitch had gone and sat on his dick without my command. She was going to regret that. The veins that ran along my shaft thumped with need. It felt hot in my hands as I gave it a steady tug. Every moan and groan those two let out only made the pre cum pool and smear over my thumb and index finger. *If she keeps going like that, I am certain I am going to nut before he does.*

Mitch didn't look a day over eighteen. A virgin. Probably had never even kissed a girl in his life, and yet there he was with his big bloody dick buried deep in my sister's puffy wet pussy. The lucky bastard. The thing was fucking huge.

I fucked myself, *slowly*. I'd coaxed him with instructions every now and again. But he had managed to find his rhythm, keeping both her and himself steady on his own. He was the best plaything we'd had since...Roe. *Fuck, I miss that cunt.* I bet she did too. So, I knew for certain that I wouldn't be letting Mitch out of my sight. Besides, if I gave her a new fucktoy, then I would get my chance to have that damn surgery.

She could waste all her energy and spare time on that boy, for all I cared. I figured, if I had him around and keep her busy, then I could finally blow my load in her without breeding some fucked up mini me into the world. The damn bitch just wouldn't let me go even half a day without fucking her again.

Ha. The poor kid has no idea what's coming.

"Rub her clit for me," I demanded. He followed without questioning, nor did he take his eyes from her swollen pussy, gloss coating her cunt and all of his shaft. *God fucking dammit, that is a tight fit.* She was in pure fucking ecstasy.

He circled his fingers over the little bud in the same rhythm that she was rolling her hips over him. He was really good at what he was doing—too good. In fact, judging by the look on her face, I'd say he was almost even better than me. *Almost.*

Watching my sister's toes curl like that from another man pleasing her needs was a euphoric sensation, seeing the mess she made—and continued to make—on that bike of his...fuck. I needed to see him do *all* of it to her again. Over, and over, and over. Until she was in a liquidated state and his mouth was fucking jawlocked.

"That's it. Now work her until she's almost ready to cum, and stop. Then I want you to stand on these pegs and fuck her from behind. Can you do that for me?" I pointed to the foot pegs of the motorbike. I wanted to see how deep he could get inside her before she folded. Make her wait for it.

"Uh, o–kay," he puffed, working her clit a little more heatedly. She whimpered and moaned as he brought her right to the edge and then left her empty, needing, and hungry.

"Good boy," I replied. I'd give credit where credit is due—he had a natural talent to tease her...and please me. Mitch stood where I asked and Twister swivelled herself around, putting her knees on the fuel tank. She leant forward so her ass pointed up and was in a firing line right to his length. She shuddered from his touch as he swirled his finger inside her, then back out. *Okay...okay, virgin. A+ for effort.*

He lined his thickly veined, shiny head right at her tight swell. Without warning she shoved herself straight against him. She cried out, almost knocking him into next Sunday.

"Deeper," I pressed. Mitch inhaled sharply through his teeth as he pushed deeper inside. "Can you feel her expanding for you?"

"God yes. Fuck."

I looked at that stunning, rose gold glimmer that flushed her cheeks. It was much more evident than usual, which was nearly sending me over the edge. *Atta boy, make that pussy pay. Take her. Make her yours.*

"Harder, Mitch," she whined. The cheeky fucking bitch. Instinctively, my fist clenched. *Mutiny.* As much as I enjoyed the sight of the guy taking her, saying his name was a *big* no-no. Only my name was to be said. She knew that. Now she was really getting under my skin. *Little fucking brat.*

I took my hand from myself, hesitantly, and tucked my thumping cock away. I would have my turn, in time—in her fucking asshole. I'd show her what happened when she broke my rules. He brought his hand around and found her clit again, grabbing her hip for a deeper impact as he thrusted. She shrieked in both pain and pleasure. Twister was leaking around him, shaking. *Fucking hell, am I going to cum without even stroking? Maybe.*

There was only one man other than *me* who could make her wet and shudder like that.

Fucking Roe.

My best friend.

My straight and narrow.

Had he been there, I would be certain that Mitch's head would be somewhere else—and not anywhere near his body. And he would be taking his place in my sister's pussy. *Rightly so.* He was good there. He was good for her. But he wasn't there. *Bastard.* She needed his blackout, menacing sex.

"Oh, fuck," I muttered under my breath. I loved the thought of her and Roe fucking again.

But for the moment, I needed to make sure she remembered who she belonged to. Now, don't peg me out to be the bad guy here. I didn't mind letting her lead loose, but she would *never* break from my chain. *I own her.* But she always knew just how to get under my skin. Flutter her eyelashes—you know that shit. Especially the twinkle in her eye she always gets after having a really good orgasm. *Fuck, she sounds good*. And fuck didn't that just make my cock throb harder. She was definitely never letting the poor son of a bitch out of her sight...if I chose to give her my good graces, that is.

I made my way beside her and gave them a few moments to come back to the here and now from his impalement, before releasing my cock again.

"Do you like the way he fucks you, sis?" I groaned as she curled her cute little hand around me. Her nails were a different shade each week, making my cock look so decorative for me. She snickered under her breath. I just knew she had some smartass remark to roll off that tongue, but she couldn't quite mutter it out.

I clutched her throat just to add to the lack of air in her chest, and her gaze grew a deviously dark shade, followed by a wicked grin. "Maybe better than you can," she choked through a moan. I furrowed my brows, holding myself together. She was really asking for it. But I'd let the guy have his moment, then I'd fuck her until she couldn't walk. When I was done, *he* could clean up the mess...for making her forget *her* place. *Fuck, and just wait until Roe is out of jail.*

"You're absolutely going to regret that," I turned a smile, matching hers and pressing my grip on her neck harder. "Oh, shit," Mitch hissed, rolling his head back, his chest panting heavily with his movements as he glided in and out of her.

"She's clenching, isn't she? When I press here." I squeezed again, both of them reacting in unison as her grip tightened on me. "Fuck," I groaned.

"Oh, no. I'm going to...where do I? Ah," Mitch cried out.

"I want you to cum on her pussy, pretty boy," I commanded. He dug his fingers into her waist and his creamy seed pooled over her ass's swollen rosy opening. Mitch groaned and shuddered with each pulsation as it trickled down her, and then the motorbike. It just kept coming.

"Good boy. Now get off, and stand there," I pointed beside her and he moved, like an obedient little puppy. "Keep your fucking ass up," I growled at Twister. *My fucking turn.*

I stood on the metal pegs and grabbed the V of her hip with one hand, collecting her hair into a knot with the other. I pulled it tightly towards me with haste, shoving her ass straight onto my very needy, pumping cock. She cooed from the pain that tore through her asshole. My nose flared at the scent of the sweet juices that smeared with the metallic bitterness of his cum, still dripping down her.

"Who do you belong to? Huh?" I hissed. She winced and stuttered. I pulled her again, harder, and she tugged even further down my shaft, making her completely inaudible. Her ass was warm and insanely tight, almost cutting the circulation off.

"Use your words, baby girl," I coaxed, my tone domineering and sharp. My balls tightened, hounding for my release. I was close to blowing. She gagged from the dull ache I was leaving in her, before finally spitting her words out. "Ah. You!" she cried out, pulling to break contact, but I held her down and made her take every inch of pain that I hammered her way.

"Yes. Me. And don't you *ever* fucking forget that." I stilled, letting the static shock of heat thread through me, filling her ass with force.

I caught my breath then let myself free of her, and smacked her on the little heart tattoo on her ass before tucking myself away. *Physically*, but not *mentally*. I glanced at the kid next to me. His face was flushed with what I could only gather was excitement and shame, his forehead shining with beads of sweat.

"Clean her up, pretty boy. And maybe—just *maybe*—I might let you have your bike back. We'll see. The fun has only just begun with you." I winked at him and he gulped down. Okay, so he didn't exactly earn my respect—yet. But he could follow my rules and every queue. I liked the kid. *For some really weird reason.*

And with that, I was on my bike and gone before either of them had the chance to process or respond.

FOUR

Twister

I TAPPED THE MESSAGE icon on my phone, addressing a new text to Drip. No words. Just the eggplant emoji and the cat face emoji, with a question mark. Drip read but didn't reply. *The fucker. This will make him think twice about ignoring me.* I opened my camera and took a picture of my tits.

"Hmm. It needs something. Delete and try again," I said to myself out loud. I collected saliva from my mouth and dribbled it out, some landing on my chest, the rest hovering over my lips.

Perfect.

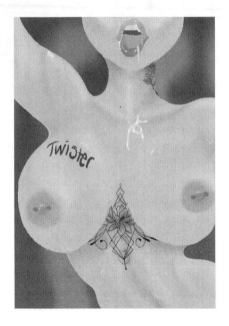

I hit send.

Drip: Jesus fucking Christ, it's 3 am, T, go to fucking sleep

Me: Can't. Come fuck me to sleep

Drip: Fine… I'll be there in 20

40 minutes later.

"Finally," I muttered to myself with a frown as I strummed my perfect little ass to the door that was thumping from the other side. *Since when does Drip knock? Why the fuck doesn't he just open it? This is his fucking house.*

I was wearing nothing but the *Gorillaz* shirt that I stole from Mitch last month. After he'd taken it off, he wiped us both clean. I was coated in cum, sweat, and blood. *Mmm, yummy.* I took his virginity *and* his money. I mean, he got my pussy, so it was only fair that I took one more thing from him to make it even, right? So yeah. I took it, and now it was mine.

I opened the door and every inch of saliva I had in my mouth suddenly dried. A tall man, built like a brick fucking shithouse leant on the pillar in black jeans, black shoes and a black hoodie on.

Leaning, and very much not moving.

Then he drew his cigarette to his mouth and the red sparkle contrasted his features. My heart fell right into my stomach. It was *not* at all who I was expecting. He was almost unrecognisable.

He had changed. *A lot.*

He was...*bigger. Terrifying?*

"Roe?" I breathed, swallowing and choking on the lump now forming in my throat. "You're not who I..." I took a small step back.

"The one and only," Roe smirked mockingly, following me into the light and blowing the ashy smoke right in my face. The white patch of hairs in his moustache followed his devilish grin. He looked livid, more rabid as he stood before the door frame...*killing me with his eyes.*

"Sorry, your brother can't make it. You'll just have to do me instead." His tone was low and enticing. He had been in jail because of me. Drip must have sent him. *How?* He had years left in his sentence for manslaughter.

A moment passed and he still hadn't moved further. The more he stared at me, the faster his chest rose and fell. *Oh, shit.* My nipples pinched with excitement.

Could he kill me? *Yes, without hesitating.*

Would he actually kill me? *Maybe.* He had enough ammo to do it. But his loyalty to my brother was the only thing stopping him.

Was I turned on? By the sheer thought of this man restricting my airways, taking my oxygen, all of my holes, and fucking me until I was either dead or unconscious...again?

Absofuckingloutley!

"Oh, what a shame." I couldn't surpass using my bratty voice. He fucking hated that. His arm was the first part of his body to barge through the doorway. I turned my brow up as he drew his hand under my shirt, his palm landing at the small of my back.

Roe tugged me forward, and with little effort, I was suddenly hard pressed against him. His muscles were hard and tight...so tight. *God fucking damn, he is huge now.* His shattered breath chilled my spine.

"It is for you. Because you won't be waking up for a while," he growled. *Don't threaten me with a good time.* I lost myself for a second in his multicoloured eyes, which had very much darkened over the years. I'd left him cold, bitter, and empty. The little ice-blue smudge in the iris of his hazel eyes that usually sparkled was now dark, filled with loathing.

He rolled his head so that his hoodie moved back and he was a little more in the light. The shadow casting over him only intensified my excited, pounding heart rate, right to my pussy. Being terrified and horny was a terrible yet delicious combination. The lighting from the doorway beaming over his face made the ivory tips of his eyelashes almost translucent, the little warmth inside made me fuzzy—for *that* part of him.

I pulled my bottom lip into my teeth and bit down lightly, throwing my gaze from his normal eye to his two-toned one, then down to his lips and taut muscles, as he peered down at me at his chest. *They are very tight under that hoodie.*

Roe was a delicious being to look at, and his fingertips felt like velvet as they trailed my spine. He somehow was a lot better looking than the last time I saw him. *Seven years ago.* The way he looked at me was as if the sight of me made his skin crawl. Which I was certain it did.

I chuckled out loud—to what, I didn't know—and he glared at me with a raised brow.

"You've lost your fucking marbles, girl, look at you," he warned. My stomach flipped in tantalisingly warm circles. Sex with Roe didn't exist. He had no real emotional connection. He was empty.

"I never had them to begin with, remember?" I whispered, holding my tongue out. Referring to when we first met, when he'd worked out that I wasn't right in the head—and fucking my brother, the youngest of the twins. I laughed again, only this time, my whole body fitted with the motion I mean, he genuinely was right. I wasn't right in the head.

"God, you're a fucking piece of work. Time to go night night."

Roe lowered his hand from my back and pinched my ass. I sighed a moan. "You always say that like it's a threat," I flirted.

"And you always think it's not" He snorted, a primal growl I hadn't heard before, sending a wave of heat over my skin. He scooped me up with little effort and used his elbow to slam the door behind him.

FIVE

Twister

"Now I CAN HAVE my moment with you. Just you and me. After seven fucking years," Roe roared, carrying me into the kitchen.

"Careful there, tiger. I can hear just how much you love me in that voice."

"How many people have you killed while I've been gone, huh?"

"Not enough," I teased. The tension in his jaw intensified.

"Daddy never loved you, did he, hmm?" Roe's voice was hateful and mocking as he threw my back against the wall, winding me on impact and wrapping his hand around me like a necklace. "Is that why you're such a little fucking killer whore? Fucking your brothers and then killing them for your own appeasement, 'cause no one fucking loves you, hmm?"

I fought for a breath but didn't reply. His hand was large enough that his thumb and middle finger touched the wall behind me, his grip crushing over my airway, but not knocking the smile from my face.

The daddy card and *the brother card? Is he trying to scare me, or make me cum?*

"Who's next on your kill list?" he hissed in my ear, sending a shudder down my spine. A moan slipped from my lips, leaving my chest empty. "Drip?" He pressed for an answer, but I didn't give one.

I clenched my jaw and smiled, the feeling of oxygen deprivation rushing to my head. Roe's lip curled, and suddenly my body was kicked out from underneath me. I landed on the floor to my knees, catching a chestful of air and feeling a dizzy spell rush to my head. Little did he know, I'd never kill Drip. I'd fucking die first. He tugged his jumper off, but as he did, the shirt underneath clung to it and went flying off with it. *Fuck.*

Looking up at him from the floor, I let my eyes wander this *new* Roe. My hungry eyes rolled along every crevice of his body. The fresh tattoos on his arms covered his piebaldism, which was a shame, really, because that's what made Roe...*Roe.* Drip had named him that when he'd first stepped foot into The Underground. Because he looked like he was always 'running on empty,' like the ink of his skin had run out during print.

"You're fucking despicable, you know that?"

"Bite me!" I moaned with a smile, washing myself in the memory of killing someone—something I'd do well to forget, but just couldn't quite seem to stay away from.

I went to inhale for a breath, but instead of air going in, a rather thick, veiny object took its place, slamming my head against the wall.

"Ah, that's better. You look better with that smile wiped off your face."

Roe was fucking pissed. Pissed that I had him put behind bars. His hand threaded my hair and he twisted, tugging it as he jolted his hips, pushing further into the back of my throat so that my skull was the only thing that stood between his cock and the wall behind me.

I could feel the warm fluid of my arousal from his aggression pooling between my thighs. I knew that he would fuck me until my body was completely depleted of movement—*and then some.* He groaned with pleasure, hissing air vigorously through his teeth as he pumped his hips into me, my head banging on the wall with each thrust. I choked and gagged as he repeated, aiming for the hilts of my throat.

I hadn't the ability for a single word around his cock. Not that I would object...but I would rather he fucked my ass or pussy—or both. I tried to ask, but it was merely an inaudible gargle.

"Have something to say, do you?" Roe panted, his chest moving rapidly as he caught his breath. I couldn't reply—*again*—so I chuckled through whatever gaps were between his shaft and my lips. He reacted instantly and shoved himself into me again, harder, tugging my head backward so that he reached further, past the flat of my tongue, while somehow lifting my body slightly up off my knees.

I coughed and strained from the pressure, but he didn't relieve me. I looked him dead in the eye, smiling with my own, staring straight into his soul, exposing my teeth slightly before lowering my gaze to his length. His nose flared.

"I'm the last person you want to piss off right now, missy. You don't have metal bars protecting you at night anymore. Not even your own brother wanted to come and fuck you. He sent me. You're fucking lucky I haven't told him about your fuck up yet," he warned. I paused...for a moment.

Why he hadn't, I didn't know. But in the mood I was in, I did not give a flying fuck. *If you're going to fuck me, then do it. If you're going to tell him, then fucking do it. If you're going to kill me, then do it.*

Just one little bite. That might get him going, then the real pain comes. I tightened my grip around him, just enough that he couldn't move back unless he wanted teeth marks on his cock. He panicked, fear in his gaze.

"Don't you fucking dare, you little bitch."

But of course, I never listen.

SIX
Drip

"HAVE YOU GOT EYELINER ready for tonight's race?" I asked my sister on the other end of the line. I called her car Eyeliner because, as cliche as it was, it was a Nissan Skyline.

It was quiet for a moment. Which was unusual for her, as she always had something to say.

"T?" I added.

She cleared her throat for a reply. "Yeah," her voice croaked. Twister sounded tired—wounded, even. She grumbled something else, but I didn't make sense of it. *Is Roe still there?* I laughed, throwing my head back in amusement, remembering why she might be cranky and *slightly uncomfortable*.

"Don't fucking start," she hissed.

"He definitely put you in your place, didn't he?"

She sighed through the speaker. *Serves her fucking right.* I was still caught up on her attitude from a month ago at our last race with Mitch. I went through a few different ideas as to what Roe might have done to her. He was rough mother fucker. Really rough. He had no willpower to stop once he was balls deep in pussy. There was no stopping him. *Period*. I didn't know how he hadn't fucked anyone to death yet. *Well, he probably has. I just don't know it.*

He had a lot of black holes in his heart, which had only worsened over the years I'd known him. Something was eating at him, that was for certain. And he'd had a sick obsession with Twister the entire time he was behind bars. Always asking how she was, where she was, how *I* was, what she was doing, who she was with. And for some reason, downright begging me put Trent in as his replacement.

Why? Well it was anyone's guess. But he was my best friend, my boy. He would tell me if something was up.

I knew he was different the second I saw that glint in his eyes, when he put two and two together. That I was in love with my sister. And to my surprise, he wanted in on it. *Great, now my dick is pulsating.*

"You're welcome, by the way," I teased.

"I wasn't thanking you."

"What is he doing back here, anyway? I thought he had more time," Twister snarled. Her usually raucous tone sounded like she was hiding a layer of fear.

I didn't usually surprise her like that, but I knew she needed that release just as much as he did. A type of release that I couldn't give her. Don't get me wrong, I *loved* bringing her pain. But she wanted...more. Roe had been in jail since the night of my brother's death, when he'd tried to kill himself. His car had cut breaks, and when it collided with a bank, of all places, he took two lives with him. Poor sods were on a nice evening stroll through the city, and they just happened to be in the wrong place at the wrong time.

So, Roe took the jump on being the driver so The Underground didn't get busted—or at the very least, pulled up for more questions for a suicide and two deaths by illegal racing. We had worked too hard to go down. His sentence, though, had been revoked early, and his bail was yesterday, based on good behaviour and sheer luck. Just in time for quite possibly the biggest race for The Underground yet.

I'd mindlessly ignored Twister for most of the day when I went to pick him up. By the time we got back, it was nearly three in the morning. An eleven-hour round trip. He was as horny as ever, and had seven years of violence, rage, and cum to fuck out. So, when I got Twister's text not long after walking in the door, I figured it was a win-win for everyone. Thinking ahead, as they say. And my sister certainly sounded like she had been very well put to sleep. Roe was good at that, when he had something to get off his chest.

My dick twitched and I cackled again, thinking of her in pain at the hands of my boy. Twister scoffed at me before hanging up with a sigh. I opened the message app, and tapped out a new one.

> **Me:** Because you're a bitch and hung up before I could get another word out. No, he doesn't have more time. The only time he needs now, is with you so he can bury his mute bat in your sassy little fucking mouth.

> **Me:** With that being said… 11 P.M. Pre-meet at the Boat Harbour. Think you can manage that, sissy? Or is that little cunt of yours too shredded?

I added a wink face and hit send, and three little dots on the bubble at the bottom appeared almost instantly.

> **Twister:** Fuck you. Cunt face

As usual, the crowd was buzzing. Cars and bikes rolled in from all angles. Minitrucks, race bikes, Harleys, fourbies, and of course the drifters in their JDM hotted up imports. Ready to take down my sister.

I rolled in on my Yamaha R7. Not my fastest bike, but I wasn't the one racing. Our nights always began with a pre-meet at a secret location. Once the money was exchanged, we then cruised to a different location for the race to avoid police and unwanted gawkers. Our club was by invite only.

The night's race would see me three hundred grand, and we hadn't even started yet. The bets were wild, for whatever reason. *No one has beaten me, and no one has beaten my sister.* Though, I had lost a thousand times to her, even though I taught her how to drift. And how to ride a fucking bike. *Damn, her on a bike is hot.*

Twister was in the middle of the parking lot, talking with someone I'd not met yet, wearing a very tight, white bralette that showed her entire midsection—*and underboob.* And she was coated entirely in purple welts. *Fuck.* She was leaning against the door of her magenta-toned Nissan Skyline R35 GTR. Of all the colours in the world, she chose that one, closest to the colour pink. She was no girly girl, but fuck she looked good in it.

Even better on it.

Mitch was there, too, standing in front of her car with his head in the engine bay. Roe was with Lachie, who had brought the tow car and trailer to take home our prize when they lost.

Twister's brown eyes followed my every movement, watching me watch the fucker before her trail his fingers over hickies. She knew exactly what she was doing. Her hand reached out behind his head, toying with the nape of his neck, bringing him in closer to her body.

He had a solid build, inked forearms. A flat cap hung on his head to the side, and he wore bright blue shorts with a lanyard hanging from the pocket. I moved slowly, sitting on my bike for a moment before shifting off in an attempt to pretend that what she was doing wasn't causing the blood in my veins to curdle with rage.

"Who's this, then?" I demanded Twister after greeting everyone else, my voice as tight as my fist. The guy swallowed hard, nervously. She moved to stand away, but I didn't take my eyes from his. I had tunnel vision.

"Zac," Lachie answered for him as he lit up a joint, the scent of weed filling the air. He gasped as I snatched the grass-filled stem out of his mouth, inhaled a hit and then planted it between the lips of Zac, trailing him up and down.

The longer he looked at me, the faster the whites of his eyes showed. His breath escalated, his eyes reading my tattoos, as if he was trying to understand me and why they were there. In particular, the snakes that looped through the skull on my neck. I didn't think I was *that* scary, but he seemed to think so.

His neck muscles worked hard as he tried swallowing again. I stepped into him, brushing chest to chest, blowing my smoke in his face as I looked down at him.

"You want to fuck my girl, pretty boy?" The note in my tone came out as a threat, but there was enough edge to sound like I was coaxing him to do so—*and immediately setting my dick off.*

"N-no," he coughed, pulling the rollie from his mouth.

"Don't lie. Look at her," I commanded as I threw his body against Twister's car. He shook his head. Roe stepped into my line of sight beside me, and something inside me lit up. Like life was back the way it was. I gripped Zac's chin firmly. He winced from the pressure of my fingers, leaving his skin indented. "Look at my sister, and tell me you don't want to fuck her."

His eyes flared, more of the whites showing. *Fuck, there it is.* The look that makes my cock solid. *My sister.* Roe chuckled, amused by the interrogation.

"Turn your fucking head and look at her," I shouted, the veins on my head protruding. By now, the crowd had circled us, watching the commotion. It was still for a split second, and Zac's head had barely moved an inch to peer over his right shoulder when the sound of a gunshot fired. Ringing silenced the scene, and my balls tightened.

I could already practically hear the excitement in Twister's head. When I looked back at her, that glow was smeared all over that slutty little face of hers, along with the blood that had splattered on her face from Roe's doing. Crimson spread over her white tee. She swiped her thumb along the droplet of blood that was trickling down her cheek and drew it between her lips.

I could feel my cock swelling. *God, she is a fucking minx.* My twisted sister. *Twister.*

○○○○

I hounded down the freeway full throttle, the adrenaline raging under my skin. I had clutched a wad of cash, revving my bike alongside Twister. She was toying with me as we took turns leading the pack. She was in a feral fucking mood from earlier. As was Roe. Whatever he did with her had gotten them both on edge. So much so that there was now a dead body in the back of Trent's BMW.

Her car flickered hues of pinks, purples, reds, yellows and blues; little LED lights ricocheting on the bitumen. My cock had been thumping at me for hours, and I was in dire need of a fucking drink. I couldn't wait to tear that pussy open—if there was any of it left, after Roe.

So much for keeping my cock on the down low. There is no way I can manage that surgery.

The race had gone the same way it did every time. No cops, no fights, *no* attention. We had run the drift through the hills, the second best spot in the state for a view of the city. The crew trailed behind me to an after party at one of my estates. My boy was back. It was time to fucking celebrate.

I opted for my beach house in Point Bay, right on the waterfront. Lachie turned off the freeway, taking the black Supra on the trailer bed to my other estate in Swan Heights, thanks to Twister's win. And the best way to thank her...was money and sex.

SEVEN

Twister

You know that little thing inside your head?

That usually sounds like a voice.

That you're supposed to listen to.

To avoid getting into situations that you shouldn't be in.

Well, I don't have one. And I always seem to catch myself in positions I am certain I wouldn't be in if I had one. There is always an itch that I can never seem to scratch when it comes to my brother. Like my sole purpose in life is to piss him off. And relish the punishments.

Was I in a right mood because Drip sent Roe over when all I wanted was him?

Yes.

Did I piss my brother off, and make him have a guy killed?

Also yes.

Was I going to keep fucking shit up and probably regretting the consequences?

Fuck yes.

'Pink Maggit' by *Deftones* blared from the speakers set up all around Drip's estate, setting the tone for the night. Just the type of music to get under my skin and electrify my nipples. Something about that slow, metal music always pinched them tight and simmered right under my skin, like it was searing.

There were at least fifty or so people in the garden with us. The rest were inside, playing pool or video games, watching porn, snorting coke of a whore's asshole, drinking, smoking, or doing whatever they could to get a hit of emotion—or to rid it.

I didn't judge. They went there to avoid that. The Underground was like the family they never had, one that welcomed them in. Rejects, weirdos, the funny lookers, the offsiders, the unwanted. Drip looked after the little city he'd built.

My brother was consumed by power, possession, control and money. But the one thing he couldn't grasp was discipline. Ironic, because he hated the word *no*. Yet he never acted on it. He didn't need to—Roe did it for him. If only he could see that Drip and I could be much more. Imagine being in such a superior position in life that, with just a click of a finger, someone would submit to your calling and take someone else's life for you.

Imagine, I couldn't. That's where our differences lay. Like I said, I was corrupted. And he wasn't.

My skin flared from the music, sending tingling waves to my clit. Hot titillation raced through my veins. The song reminded me so much of Drip and I, because I was his dirty little whore, and we were the leaders of it all. He and Roe were in the spa next to me, being absolute fucking idiots, trying to tap each other's beer bottles on the tops to froth them.

"Drip?" I cooed, keeping my tone of voice low and sensual, like a prissy slut. He pulled his attention from Roe in a what-does-this-needy-bitch-want-*now* kind of reaction. His eyes narrowed at the lip I was biting *in that way*. I knew how to get under my brother's skin, and he always let me.

There was just something about the "wrong" that I was compelled by. That *need* for the friction. It didn't matter if it was his command to *fuck* someone else or to fuck *in front* of someone. Begging to make someone bleed for *my* pleasure, or bleeding for some*one's* pleasure. The lust for blood. If it was wrong, I had to do it.

I needed *his* control. I was his, gladly. Inside and out. And he needed to make sure that I—and everyone he let touch me—knew that.

I closed my eyes for a moment, but that impish grin that liked to mark my face returned, once again provoked by that need for friction.

"I was thinking. We haven't raced each other in...fuck, how long has it been?" I teased, then posed for a selfie on Snapchat, completely ignoring that I was still covered in blood. Going by the growl that rumbled under his breath, my comment pierced his skin on impact. I knew well and good when our last race together was. But the fucker had to pay some way or another for not fucking me when I had begged him.

I made sure to emphasise the position of my phone for ultimate cleavage, and the perfect "fuck me face". I hit send and looked at my brother.

His jaw was tense. *Good, it worked. That might ruffle his feathers.* Roe shook his head in disapproval and his nose flared, the darkness in his eyes suddenly a shade darker. Except for the bright blue patch.

"I don't *need* to race you." The tone of his voice was etched with denial and temerity.

"You better shut your fucking mouth, before I shove something hard in there and tell the world your dirty little fucking secrets until all you can gargle out is nothing but spit and cum. You've caused enough trouble tonight. We don't need any more of your fucking shit," Roe added, trying to cloak the anger in his words. *Don't need any more? Oh, you fucking fool...do you not remember that that only entises me more? I'll fucking give you more.*

"Aww, is the big, tough boy getting mad?" I teased.

But he wasn't just talking about earlier...I had left a mark on his cock the night before, and he made me pay for it. And yet he still hadn't slipped up my secret yet—*killing my brother.* Even though Roe was furious, I bet he was hard. As if the night before wasn't enough...four times. *Four fucking times.* And hickies from my neck to my clit. Everything hurt, but that didn't stop me. Nothing did.

Roe's variegated face showed nothing but intrigue and mischief. I knew that if I kept pissing him off, he was going to eventually tell Drip the real reason our brother, Phantom, died. But in pure Twister style, I never listen to that inside voice that's *supposed* to stop you from doing stupid shit.

I giggled, pushing my tits out a little more for another photo and hit send. I had the two of them perplexed, especially Drip. I kept swinging in the egg chair that hung from the ceiling and clutched my phone between my thighs to open the cap of a bottle of Bacardi. I let the liquid burn my throat in delicious torrents as it went down, heating my entire body as it reached my stomach. *Like fuel to the fucking fire.*

"Ah," I swallowed another sip. "So...do you think he could outdrift me?" I pressed again in a whiny voice, laughing even louder than before. Drip grumbled under his breath again. He hated the fact that I was a better driver than him. He taught me how to drive, and Phantom. The last race Drip and I had was only hours before our brother died. All three of us, side by side. Drip hadn't raced me since.

I jolted to a sudden intrusion of pleasure that strung at my clit; a notification dinged on my phone. I swiped to see a little fire emoji with Mitch's cartoon avatar face highlighted over the photo on Snapchat. He'd liked the pictures I sent him. I saw the little signal that he was typing, and then another notification buzzed. A photo of his helmet with the visor flipped open and the heart emoji eyes filled my screen, and a title spread across the image saying "Jesus take the wheel. I'm on my way."

He'd gone with Trent to do whatever it was with the body, but at least he was coming. I liked having him around.

Drip cleared his throat and I tilted my head to look at his narrowed eyes on mine. "You're digging yourself a bigger hole, T," he warned.

"What are you gonna do about it, hmm?"

"Ohhh, bro. Let me at her, please!" Roe begged him with a sinister laugh. He was more furious than earlier, now that I had brought up Phantom. It made my nipples tighten again.

"What do we do then, boss?" Drip played, aiming his question to Roe but staring straight at me. I gulped. Was he going to put Roe in charge? Really? *Shit.* For a split second, I thought of what would happen if he told him. Drip would disown me. But it was only a split second.

Roe leapt out from the spa, his erection on full display through his soaked, waterlogged jeans. I jolted upright as he grabbed the swinging egg, forcing the air to gasp from my mouth. He lifted it higher, so that I was tilted at a ninety-degree angle and slipping further down the chair. Roe shook it vigorously, leaving me no choice but to fall against his chest.

He groaned as I wrapped my legs around him, the tattoo above his eyebrows following his frown. "What to do. What to do with this tedious little thing? Fucking the bitch is only going to reward her for being one," Roe said to Drip as he knotted a section of my hair in his hand. He tugged my head back and the heat of his breath hounded down my neck, a direct link to my pussy.

"Teach this *slut* a lesson or two, seeing as me fucking you unconscious wasn't enough. Let's see how much that pussy can handle when you can't cum." His arousal and loathing filled the air.

I giggled at his tormenting words, the excitement of whatever idea he had only intoxicating my head. The man hated me with such passion that he wouldn't hesitate to put a bullet in my head, nor feel an inch of remorse. The only thing stopping him was my brother. Roe was the best hate fuck a girl like me could ever ask for. He could fuck you to death, and you'd do nothing but love him for it, begging for more.

"There is definitely something wrong with that fucking head of yours," he grumbled.

And with that, he carried me out into the garden.

EIGHT

Drip

THE BUZZ OF BEER had lightened my core. *Or am I still on a high from seeing my boy kill for me again?* Either way, I was hyped—and horny as fuck. Roe had something up his sleeve, and I was all for it. He was in charge. And I got the feeling that I wouldn't be disappointed.

I had a few ideas of what he might do. He had been behind bars for seven years, so whatever rage and hateful sins he had locked up along with him were just hounding to come out. Particularly towards Twister.

I followed Roe and Twister to the garden where everyone else was fraternising, the old oil drums lit with fire illuminating the area. He signalled something to the DJ, and then 'A Good Day To D13' by *Arankai* played, the volume upping many notches. *Oh? Interesting.* There were a few plastic chairs scattered throughout the yard that no one was sitting on, and a table beside the DJ with an assortment of drugs and alcohol on ice in the esky. You know…the usual. Everyone had stopped what they were doing to watch whatever shit was about to go down. Some from earlier, some tagalongs. Most knew how dangerous Roe was, having seen it face to face.

He stopped adjacent to one of the firepits and lowered her to the ground without letting her go entirely. He grabbed a chair and threw it beside her, gesturing his finger to sit.

"Sit," he commanded. *Oh, this is going to be good.* She loved a crowd. She sat on the chair eagerly, looking up at him through her eyelashes. She looked so sultry and beautiful like that, submissive and in total admiration of what Roe was dishing out, awaiting whatever punishment was going to come her way.

While two other people took a few bags from the table, I took one of the rollies and another beer from the cooler and pulled a chair under me, sitting on it backwards. I leant my arms over the top to watch on. I tittered as Roe lit a cigarette, his face filled with amusement and anticipation. My cock throbbed with excitement. He was definitely up to something.

I lit my rolly, the scent of the rich green haze filling my nose with the cloud of smoke that followed. *Intoxicating.*

"Who's first?" Roe shouted over the music to the crowd, scanning everyone as he spun in a circle. Everyone's faces whitened a shade or two in pure panic and terror. A turn of my sister without my permission? They knew better. *Immediate game over.* And just as I expected, no one chirped up. "No one?"

Roe roared through a blow of smoke, taking it upon himself to pace the crowd for a suitable opponent to play with. Twister sat with her legs crossed on the chair, her smile cracked sideways in anticipation, and I just knew for certain that she was soaked under those tight little shorts. *Fuck, she just knows how to turn a man on.*

"You," Roe pointed his cherry red cigarette at a familiar face; a good-looking, middle-aged man in track pants and a tight black motorbike thermal top. His toned physique flexed through the fabric. He had been hanging around in our club for a few years now. Not new, but not old. He knew his place. He'd never once indicated trouble. He threw his hands up in the air in denial but Roe wouldn't take no for an answer.

"Take her shirt off," he commanded.

"What?"

"You heard me," he growled. He was in his element. I wondered if he was like that in jail. Boss. *This is such a fucking turn on.* The man thrashed his head around as if he was looking for someone, and then finally his eyes found mine. He shook his head again and I shrugged my shoulders. He knew that Twister was *my* girl, and those who touched her without my say so ended up in a plastic bag. The only person who existed on this earth who didn't need it, was Roe.

The next song started to fade in—'Next Contestant' by *Nickelback*. *How fucking ironic.* Cash made its course around the crowd; the fuckers were placing their bets. I smiled, laughing under my breath. The man passed Roe and stood before Twister, gently hovering his hands over where her bloody crop top sat on her chest. She looked up at him with a look that only made your dick twitch and your balls tighten. He was tall, so the arc of her neck protruded as it bent back to look at him, the rose tattoo on her neck only adding to her in the lighting. *Jesus fucking hell.* He curled his fingers under the fabric and lifted barely a fraction before hestating and looking at me again, then Roe, then Twister.

"Come on, we all want to see those big perky tits. Don't we?" Roe coaxed the crowd, some perking up to woo, whistle or shout while others chose to stay silent. And in one swift movement, the little tee was up, over her head and on the ground. There was not an inch of skin on her boobs that didn't have a hickey. Her nipple piercings sparkled and her eyes lit up like a christmas tree, feeding off everyone's eyes on her. She fluffed her hair and shifted in a way that made her body arch a little more, pulling her midsection even tighter.

That fucking body.

My cock was hounding me, so I had to adjust it to release some of the pressure.

"Good, now fuck off," Roe shrilled. The man was quick on his feet and ran off somewhere the eye couldn't see. "Who wants a turn of the boss's girl next, then, uh?"

Me. I wanted a turn with *my* girl. I was itching for her, but I wanted to see where Roe was going with his display. It took everything I had to pull myself back and not fuck her there and then. Especially with that face she was giving Roe; she was fucking begging for it.

He pulled another man who was standing behind someone else. This one had more fear on his face than the last. Younger, and a hell of a lot more timid than the last. I'd only seen him around once before, so I wasn't certain if he knew *the rules*.

"Take her shorts off."

The blonde-haired guy proceeded to do exactly as he was told without objecting, though his body was clearly fighting a war he wouldn't win. When he was done with her shorts, he blew a sigh of relief and went to walk back to where he was, but Roe stopped him in his tracks. "You're not done yet," he paused. *Oh? Go on...*

"Tell us how wet she is," Roe called. *Mmm, fuck.* I shifted in my seat, letting that friction of my wet pants do something to my cock. "With your tongue," he added.

"But—" the man projected, pure terror laced in his tone. But he was very quickly interrupted by the sharp yank of his head from Roe tugging his hair backward. Like there was nothing to him, the guy was on his knees. "Ahh," he whimpered.

"It was *not* a fucking question," Roe hissed. I was certain that a bit of spit left his mouth. *Fuck me dead. I am going to cum soon if he keeps going.*

Roe's jeans were swollen at the seams, his impressive erection just begging to come out...as was mine. Twister's chest panted with each breath, her lip between her teeth, chewing hungrily with need. The guy again hesitantly began Roe's command, shuffling along his knees before Twister. A tear trickled down his cheek, as though he knew his life was about to diminish. Maybe he did know the rules. His hand slowly crept along her thigh and turned in towards the arc of her pelvic area. He paused for a moment. I was certain the man was either going to cum or pass out. *Both, I hope.*

"Mhmm, yes. Pull them aside,"

He stilled again for a moment. "Am I really going to have to repeat myself?" Roe said as he grabbed his hair again.

"Ahh. N-no," he whimpered. The fair-haired male began to slowly roll his two fingers in under the fabric of her G-string and gasped, shuddering instantly. That was usually the reaction people had when they touched her pussy. No doubt, she was absolutely fucking soaking.

Twister's body language shifted instantly, and she turned her attention to me with a shit eating grin that scrunched up her perfect little nose. *Oh, shit.* She was definitely in a real fucking mood.

I didn't think I had ever seen her eyes that...dark.

Sinister.

Why does that only make my cock throb more?

NINE
Drip

SHE STRUMMED HER BROW at me before fixing her eyes back on the man on his knees before her. She inched his mouth closer to the heaven between her legs before holding the man there in place with the grip of her thighs.

She swayed her hips as he rolled his tongue up the slit, and then peered at me yet again for a brief second. The whites of her teeth peeked from her lips. A husky, evil laugh followed as she positioned her hands to either side of his head. *No...she wouldn't?*

She did.

Fuck.

The sounds of bones crunching filled the air and then echoed over the silence in the garden. What an imperfectly perfect moment for a song to change over. Silence.

That's my girl. I shouldn't have been thinking that, but fuck. His lifeless body slid down her leg and bundled to the floor, everyone suddenly wide-eyed and still, weary. Twister's rusty giggle was the only sound bouncing through the air as she squatted down to grab his hand. She rolled her neck and inserted his fingers in her mouth, slurping up her juices off his flesh.

Why is the only thought in my head the desire to fuck her, and then blow my load on the guy...in the guy?

The dead guy.

I knew I was fucked up for even thinking that. But in my defence, my sister was worse.

My twisted sister. A moment or two passed and I caught sight of Mitch. I didn't know exactly how long he had been there—I assume long enough to have seen the whole thing, given how fucking pale he was. *Fuck, this is just getting better and better.* I quickly darted over to him and shoved him in front of me and got walking.

"You're coming with me, pretty boy."

"Bu-wh—"

"Shh," I demanded. He didn't respond or resist. We stayed out of Twister's line of sight and started walking to the house.

"You're sick, you know that?" I heard Roe's tone through a smile as he growled at her. I looked over my shoulder and his whole body was practically putting her in incognito as he leant over the chair.

"I believe the term you are looking for is *twisted*," Twister snarled at him playfully, clearly very pleased with her efforts. I pulled out my phone and dialled Trent's line. The last thing I needed was people lurking around a dead body under my name.

"Boss?" he hollered down the speaker.

"I need you in the garden—Point Bay," I replied, not taking my grasp off of Mitch.

"On it," he sounded, and then the line went dead. Trent was one of my headmen. His role was purely the terminator. If there was trouble, he dealt with it. I never questioned what he did or how he did it. He stepped up when Roe left for a stroll behind bars. He was no Roe, though. Roe was a wickedly sick fucker; he didn't just *kill*... he violated. If you could think of someone dying in the most inhumane way possible, double it, light it on fire, piss on it, then double it again. But that was just what happened in The Underground. And people would do well to remember that. It was my fucking club. My city. My rules. If you fucked up, there were consequences.

Roe scooped Twister up over his shoulder like she was a little doll.

A breedable doll. One day, sis... one day.

She went willingly, like the good girl she was. As he carried her towards us in the house, I noticed her ass was laced in more welts, red and purple scabs. She still hadn't learnt her lesson. Roe tugged at her G-string, tearing the fabric and throwing it on the grass. "Oh," I moaned quietly as he snagged two fingers through her slit, collecting her wet arousal. He groaned as he swiped one of his digits over his tongue, licking it like a lollipop.

"Killing someone turns you on, does it? By the taste of you, I'd say yes." He said impishly, though it wasn't a question.

"I'd only be lying if I told you it didn't," she replied in a way that made me flush with immense heat under my skin.

"You're right...you are twisted. Now what is your *brother* going to do with a dead body, hmm?" Roe asked, finishing off the question with a spank on her ass, leaving behind a pink handprint over the little heart tattoo she had on her cheek and adding to the other wounds.

She breathed out a little whimper, and then a giggle. Her pussy was coated in the glistening shine of her arousal. Roe stopped eye to eye with me and winked, keeping me out of her sight. He looked at Mitch and then placed his still-wet finger before my lips.

I froze for a split one of a second, a flutter in my stomach pacing. *Okay, this is new.* If I let him do that, it would be the most intimate that Roe and I had ever been. But the scent of her cunt roared up my nose, and without thinking a second more, I let his thick finger push past my teeth. I twirled my tongue around it mindlessly, tasting every last drop of Twister, her gloss mixed with a hint of salty sweat and stained cigarette. He inserted another and used his thumb to press up against the base of my tongue under my jaw. I really should have felt emasculated in the situation, but I didn't.

"He's a big boy. He will figure it out," she toyed. She had no idea we were behind her.

God, I can't wait to pull these jeans off and let my cock throb without restriction. Seeing her take someone's life because they touched my property without my permission only made me more fucking impatient. It built the need to fuck her. I wanted to praise her for her loyalty yet punish her for bringing up Phantom. *Tonight has already been so fucking wild, can it even get any better?* With Roe in charge, though, I was pretty certain it could.

"Yes. He is a big boy. But you're not getting him to fuck your brains out tonight."

TEN

Twister

God, I COULD JUST *about fucking die*. Everything in my body was screaming.

My skin was on fire.

My pussy was throbbing.

My belly was *aching* to be rearranged, and my back was in dire need of being blown out.

It had been a while since I fucked someone's life up. Seven years, to be exact. The sound of his last breath only made my orgasm inch closer. And the way Drip looked at me only intensified it. I was fucking dripping in sex.

And now that very climax was begging to come out, considering Roe had just swirled his fingers over my clit. *The fucker.* One more circle and I'd explode—or less than, even. But I had the feeling that he wasn't taking me inside to play with my pussy unless I did whatever it was he desired. Not that I'd complain.

And where the fuck is Drip? I hadn't seen him after I killed the other guy.

*Jesus, that itch...*I felt as though I had only scratched the surface. *I want more...so much more.*

"If I told you I *didn't* want my brains to be fucked out, would you do it out of spite?" I pushed in a childish manner. He cackled but offered nothing. I huffed and went back to being the brat that I inevitably told myself I was. A murderous brat, at that. I mentally drew a crown to my head. *I dub thee, Queen Murderer.*

I could hear the sounds of moaning and muffled shouting—and spanking?—echoing from the hallway. We reached the entrance of one of the entertainment rooms upstairs, where the pool table and pinball machines were. Roe slammed my back onto the felt green pool table, where I could see everyone else in the room. Some were hanging beside the bar talking, others just sitting on the couch in front of the screen. *But no Drip.* "Where's my brother?" I asked, with no reply.

There was a bar in the corner, and the pull-down cinema screen was playing porn at an electrifying volume. My pussy clenched seeing four masked men dressed in war cosplay like Call of Duty, their cocks out with shining tips. One was wanking and a girl tied up on a chair. They were roleplaying, as if she was the villain. I hadn't seen that type of porn before. It was fucking hot. *Masked men...fucking yes. Can I be her? Can I be in *her?*

"Be a good little slut for me, won't you? Stay," Roe commanded, his tone low and in control. I rolled my eyes and put my fingers between my slit. "No. You will fucking not." He ripped my arms up above my head, knotting my wrists together with the pool ball pocket. "Fucking. Stay."

Roe opened the bar and pulled out a bottle of Sambuca and a tripod stand. He drank several gulps straight from the bottle, and then set up the tripod on the floor before me. He pressed his phone onto the stand and tapped a few buttons, and then I was on the cinema screen, replacing the porn. Roe strolled over to the window that overlooked the garden we had just come from, pointing a remote downward. Screen sharing to the DJ's screen, no doubt. *Of course.*

I felt warm liquid trickle down my leg. It was getting hot, and my skin was roaring with flames. He split a devilish smirk, which only intensified the feelings I had. Whatever he was planning was getting me wetter by the second.

"Now what?" I pressed in a hissy, impatient tone, my legs becoming more restless the more I clenched them together to lull the throb between them. I tugged at the taut strings around my wrists, but they didn't budge.

But my attitude only confirmed he was doing exactly what he wanted to: piss me off and tease me. *Fucking hell.* I was going to have to up the ante.

"Now you wait."

"For what?" I snarled. Roe knew how to get under my skin, and he knew I hated waiting. "For your brother." He groaned the words, sending a chill up my spine.

Roe laughed from the pit of his chest. I propped my head up to see Mitch under Drip's grip, muted by his hand. He looked absolutely fucking terrified. *Of me?* Very opposite from the last time he saw me.

"Well, isn't this going to be interesting," Drip sneered as he nudged Mitch into the room a little further.

"What are you going to do to me? I don't want any trouble." He protested in a panic.

"I think it's more what you're going to do to me," I said to Mitch playfully. He gulped nervously as Roe approached me.

"Yeah, but... what about the other guy?" Mitch added.

"Don't worry, pretty boy, we just want to play." Roe ran his finger from the crevice between my collarbones and up my neck to my chin, following the trails of hickies that he had left over my skin the night before. My back involuntarily rose, arching off the pool table as a moan fell from my lips. I panted as I lowered myself in his absence.

"She needs an attitude adjustment." He squeezed my cheeks, his grip firm.

"Ah," I winced.

"You see, kid, the fucking bitch brought up our brother, Phantom. Who is very fucking dead right now. So, of course, she needs a reminder of what happens when *he's* mentioned."

"Say. Fucking. Less." Roe hissed.

The two of them bickered over me like they both knew my crime. But Roe was the one who had the vendetta. He had a real reason to plot revenge. Drip was just mad that I brought up the past, and his dead brother.

I saw Mitch's face, all signs of panic and nerves, yet...that fucking bulge in his pants. Drip grabbed one of the pool cues from a bystanding male who was stunned and fully focused on my pussy. *I guess it did have a habit of causing this reaction.* Drip held the cue out at arms-length, the tip of it pressing under my chin so that it left me no choice but to squirm. I moaned from the touch, and my breath escalated.

He trailed the cue down my neck, stopping at my nipple and circling the chalk end around it. My already taut skin reacted and pinched tighter from the sensation. I sighed as he pulled it away.

"Here, take this," he demanded Mitch, holding out the cue for him. After a moment of hesitation, he grabbed it. Colour was still absent from his face, yet a wet patch had formed over his cream pants.

"Do you think you can make her cum without fucking her or rubbing this on her clit?" Roe pried.

"I...what? I-I don't know," Mitch responded, his voice cracking like a pubescent teenager, just like last time. My skin sparked with goosebumps, more moisture dripping down my ass crack for his innocence. I had his virginity and he was still frigid.

"Come on, you've seen that pussy before. What happened to that loyal little puppy I saw last time?" Drip added in a hoarse whisper. "The one who did *everything* I told him, like good boys do."

"But...th-that wasn't in front of lots of people. A-and she just killed...and what about the other guy from earlier—"

"Oh, pretty boy," Drip tsked, cutting him off. "That's what happens when I don't give permission to touch my sister." He laughed. "People die."

I gnawed at my lip. It was Drip's way of toying with our playthings. Teasing, instructing and pushing boundaries. Caught between possessive and obsessive ownership over me and having the desire to share me with whomever he wished. A total mind fuck that I loved.

"But not me, right?" Mitch squeaked in a panic. He tried to take a step back, but Roe stood behind him like the meanest looking bodyguard.

"Sure...let's go with that," Roe tormented. *This is going to be interesting, Roe has never been in charge. And he's certainly never been the dominant partner when we are all together.*

"Now. I want you to get her *this* close." Roe pinched his fingers together. "And then stop. Oh, and smile, because everyone can see you."

ELEVEN

Drip

I KNEW FOR CERTAIN it wasn't going to take long before a pool of jizz soaked through my jeans. Mitch was already covered in his own precum and Twister was tied up, lying in a fucking ocean. Her gorgeous fucking pink glossy pussy was beaming on every fucking TV screen inside and outside. *This is turning me on too much.*

I had no idea where Roe was going with it, and the excitement had my cock throbbing. And adding the kid into the middle of it just made it more electric. *If* I could manage to hold out from taking over, that is.

"But he hasn't given me permission? Only you have, and that's not the rules," the kid muttered to Roe under a fallen breath, tremoring with the stick in his hand. If I was in command, he wouldn't be shaking like that.

"That's right," I added.

"So who am I supposed to obey? Because if I go one way, I'm a dead man, but if I go the other, I'll be even deader."

"Well, hey, I don't mind killing you if you say no to either of us. Why don't you just stop fucking talking and follow our rules, eh?" An untamable demeanour charged over Roe's face. Jail fucked him up big time, so I couldn't be certain whether he would hurt the kid or not. There was already another dead body on my lawn. I wasn't overly keen on the idea of another to clean up. Besides, the kid was supposed to be keeping my sister entertained. *Yeah, because that plan is going so well.*

"Fine," Mitch muttered. Roe sat on the edge on the couch, gesturing his hand out toward Twister.

"But...remember, she can't cum. That's her punishment for being a fucking bitch. If you do make her cum, then I'll fuck you. Don't tempt me, I've been in jail. I know how tight a virgin man's asshole is."

I leant against the bar and watched Mitch as he lowered the pool stick down her tight little body, listening to her moan and squirm as he trailed further down. The angle of the camera was prime, zoomed in enough so that you could see every clench. My cock throbbed for what was mine, but I eagerly waited for Roe's plan to unfold.

It took a moment for Mitch to find his place, but he eventually pulled his head into the right mind space to focus. *Good boy.*

Make that pussy throb and swell for us. I was begging to praise him.

Twister was barely holding it together, and so was I. She was digging her sharp claws, painted the same colour as her car, straight into the fabric of the pool table. Mitch tormentingly drew the cue everywhere over her body *but* the area she wanted it.

He took the liberty of drawing the stick to the rough fabric of the table. He rubbed it aggressively before planting it back onto her skin again. The three of us sharply drew in a breath in unison at the sounds that Twister was making as the burning touch seared over her skin. Mitch's tactic was leaving behind a slight hue of pink wherever the cue trailed, marking her. *Friction.*

I wasn't certain exactly how much time had passed. Watching my sister arch her back, squirm against her restraints, moan and pant to be touched the way she was begging for seemed to have a funny effect on time. So I had no fucking clue how long it had been, but it was long enough for her to be covered in sweat, *almost* in tears.

"Yeah. Atta boy. Look at her, she's fuckin' wrecked. Now, ask the slut to beg for you to let her release."

The kid nodded at Roe, then looked straight into her eyes. He cleared his throat and swallowed. At first the words didn't come out when he opened his mouth. "Beg me to let you cum."

He said it like a question, not an order. *He has much to learn.* Twister's lips separated to speak, but Roe cut her off.

"No. Again. And hold your head up."

Mitch turned to look at me—for approval, I suppose. As much as I wanted to give it to him, I was a man of my honour. Roe was the boss tonight.

I kept my glare on Mitch cold, leaving him nothing but his own thoughts. He turned back to Roe, then Twister, adjusting his very swollen bulge under his clothes.

"Beg me to let you cum," he repeated, much stronger than the last. *That's my boy.*

"Please. Please," Twister pleaded through chattering teeth. She was trembling with a need for release. Mitch made a funny little noise, like a whimper. No doubt, he was only moments away from blowing his load. *Hold it in just that little bit more, pretty boy.* I wanted—no, *needed*—to see him fucking her again. *If* Roe would allow it.

"Nope. Not today, bitch," Roe declared, finishing the snark with a sinister laugh. *Fuck.* He really had it in for my sister. He was never going to let her cum, only giving her the impression that she could earn it, then letting her down. The sigh of rejection that rolled off Twister's tongue only boiled my blood. I hated hearing her that way, defeated and denied.

I took a breath to regain focus, tuning into the scene around me. One guy on the couch had cum all over his stomach, watching Twister on the screen, while the other guy was still going at it. I assumed the rest had left. I hadn't the ability to even bother looking outside.

Roe grabbed the stick off Mitch and put it to his mouth. "Spit," he ordered, and Mitch dropped a bubbly sample of saliva onto the tip of the wooden rod. Roe then lowered it straight onto Twister's clit.

"Mmm—aah," she cried out to the sudden punch of pleasure, but Roe took it away immediately, putting a halt to the climax that had been lingering, denied time and time again.

"Again," he growled, with the stick to Mitch's mouth again, his tone a little weaker than before. *How long is Roe going to last before he gives in and fucks her until she either throws up or blacks out?* Mitch spat onto the stick again and Twister cried louder in its presence, but was still left empty and panting.

Roe repeated this *eleven more fucking times,* causing the lump that was lodged in my throat to swell, and my fists to tighten with more angst. Sweat continued to pour from her skin, and her entire body trembled with desperation. Twister was left unable to mutter the word *"please"* anymore.

It took everything in my body not to swing my fist at Roe, fucking her there and now to relieve her, *and me.* But I didn't.

"What do you want, slut? Tell us. Use your fucking words."

She stirred and panted as a reply to him, then the stick came plummeting with great force against her stomach and tit. Right over the line of hickies. She cried out, and in one swift movement he rolled her onto her front, then yanked her down the table by her ankles. Twister's shoulders strained against the restraint, and Roe took the cue to her skin again, harder. An astronomical brand of elevated pink and bruised red surfaced her skin. She lifted her ass up for more, heaving whimpers of need. Her pussy pulsated like she was signalling morse code to my cock, and the clear liquid of heat dripped from her like a fucking tap.

"Have you learnt your lesson?" he asked as he snapped the cue clean in half over his knee.

"Mhm," Twister moaned in defeat.

"That's what I thought."

He dragged the sharp end of the stick along the mark it had left on her skin. She winced, but there was an abundance of pleasure under those sweet lips. Faint white lines followed the stick down to her ankles, where he discarded the last piece of the snapped cue onto the floor.

Without hesitation, in one swift movement, Roe got onto the table and pumped his rock solid cock straight into her. She gagged as he impaled her. *Fuck, I am going to cum in my jeans.* He thrust into her without mercy until her climax surfaced again, and then he pulled himself out, leaving her empty once more. He smacked her on the ass and laughed, then leapt off the table. How he didn't nut there and then was anyone's guess.

"God fucking hell," I groaned, looking at her with her ass up in the air, her face flat on its side, swollen and ready. She was taking it so well, accepting her punishment. *My fucking good girl.*

"Your turn," Roe nodded his head to the kid, staring straight at the bulge that was hard pressed against his pants, leaking and throbbing. His face turned whitewash again. I wanted to see him fuck her again and by the look on his face, there was no fucking way he was going to do it.

"But—" Mitch protested.

"Now!" Roe shouted. I flinched slightly. He meant business. *Shit, am I scared of him, too?* It was hot. Mitch was quick to jump up onto the table, getting to his knees and placing himself at her entrance. Her breath shattered as he hovered there, waiting for the next que, or his death—whichever came first. Despite all that, the kid's dick was still as solid as ever, gambling with his life. Or so he thought. I wouldn't actually kill him. *I don't think.*

"No! I'm fucking playing your games, man. This is too much, I was cool about it at first, but come on," Mitch screeched, pulling away and tugging his pants up. My eye twitched involuntarily. I didn't like disobedience, especially when it came to my sister. But I wasn't the one in command. I clenched my fist and held my tongue, my piercing clinging to the roof of my mouth. I rolled it around to distract myself to my best ability. *Trust Roe's judgement. He's in charge tonight. Let him have his way. You owe him that, at least.*

But alas, I could not.

"You don't *want* to fuck my sister?" I spoke through grit teeth, pulling back the anger inside me.

"No!" he bit back in a cold tone. *Such lies.* Twister's soft little whimper of rejection stung me as it howled into my ear again, ten times worse than the last. I couldn't hold back anymore. I was convinced I was put on this earth to protect her. My possession.

I was her protector.

I was all she had.

I took her under my wing to keep her safe in life. She'd been denied her whole fucking life. Be fucking damned if I was going to let her be rejected by anything or anyone ever again.

Fuck Roe. I'm the fucking King.

I don't know how, but I managed to move from where I was standing, suddenly having my hand clamped in a bundle of Mitch's shirt and his face in mine.

"Fuck. Her," I spat at the kid. My skin was on fucking fire. Watching him chew on his words made my balls taut.

"No!" he squeaked. The shine of a tear formed under his eyelid. Those puppy dog eyes conveyed total confusion.

I laughed insincerely and rolled my neck in frustration. I took a step back for a breath before I did something I would regret, but did not release him from my grip. *No one says no to that pussy. No one says no to me.* I locked onto his pale hazel eyes, and softened mine.

"Do you think I'm going to kill you?"

He clenched his jaw. "Y-n-yes," he muttered.

"I see. But, you want to please me right?"

"Yes," Mitch sighed after a pause.

"And you want to please her?"

"I do." He softened like butter. Because he knew I wouldn't kill him. Twister liked him too much. Shit, I liked him too much. I knew he wanted to please me. He wanted to prove his loyalty to her and I. Roe just got a little too far under his skin. I had to give the kid credit; he'd done a fucking brilliant job so far.

"Good, then please me. Please me by letting her pussy milk that pretty cock of yours."

Twister reacted with a breathy moan, her pussy pulsating to my very words. I leaned forward, tugging his pants down and freeing his cock. Without thinking, I wrapped my palm around it, letting the heat of his hard-working veins sear my skin. I froze for a split second, having never had another man's length in my hand before, but in the heat of the moment, I kept going. I peeled his foreskin slowly over the head and collected his precum under the skin before pulling back down again. He groaned, tremoring slightly under my hand. I directed his wet tip at my sister's swollen hole. "She's all yours. Claim her."

He sharply drew in a breath through his teeth in what I could only note as ecstasy as he pushed himself in. A tight fit, the skin at her entrance taut and pale.

"Good boy. I need to see her tight little pussy clench around all of you. Can you do that for me? And then you can release." I breathed.

He nodded mindlessly. The boy was speechless. Twister leant back against him as he filled her. He glided in and out of her, leaving a sheen coating over his cock every time he pulled out, right to the tip.

The sounds of my sister's enjoyment thrilled me to the point that I had no choice but to palm my cock and stroke slowly down my shaft, my thumb sliding over the wet tip like I had with Mitch's. I let out a sigh of relief as I tugged back a layer of tension.

I had no fucking control.

I could not go a fucking second more without fucking myself while watching my sister get railed.

TWELVE
Twister

"FUCK," I SHOUTED WITH whatever air was left in my chest, tightening my fist into a ball over the cotton knots of the ball net. It was pure fucking torture. I was aching for a release. *When I get done with this fucking shit, I am going to shove my foot so far up Drip's ass, he'll have my pretty little fucking toes for teeth. Why in the fuck did he put Roe in charge?*

"Just—FUCK!" I screamed. I was so fucking exhausted. And mad.

So fucking mad. I just wanted to cum, was that so fucking hard? I was so fucking close. Just a little faster, a little harder.

Roe was *exactly* like Drip's twin, Phantom. The delinquent, and too fucking cocky for his own good. He was all dick and no brain.

I winced at the memory. *Keeping secrets*...but those memories were only meant for *my* grave, never to be pulled from my darkened, corrupt, forbidden soul.

89

Drip tried so hard to be like him, to be him. But his backbone was made of butter, not a steel rod like Phantom had. That was why he could never hold back from me; he could never edge me for long enough. Not like Phantom. Not like Roe.

Drip thought I was the needy one, but he couldn't go longer than a few days without fucking me—believe me, we'd tried. Practice for castration surgery and all. *What a fail*. I wanted a gutful of his cum more than anything I had ever wanted, but without the added accidents that come with breeding.

Not again.

I shrugged the haunting memory aside.

I wondered if Drip was giving Roe the lead because maybe, just maybe, it felt like having his brother back in his life again. Jail had definitely done a number on him. I mean, he was still Roe, but more...numb, fearless and...unwired. There was something in him that both terrified me and enticed me at once. I couldn't tell if he was going to take revenge on me for killing one of his two best friends and not telling my brother about it, or make me pay for my choices for the rest of my life.

"Ah," I moaned, everything inside me tightening, but my release was just out of reach. I pushed back for more, but Roe perked up again. *Fuck off*.

"Okay. That's enough, big boy. Out you come!" he demanded. His voice was low and barbaric. "No, please no," I sighed as my pussy slowly emptied, but was left ignored. *Jesus fucking*

Christ, what is with this cunt? With my forehead planted on the green of the table, exhausted and confused, all I could hear behind me was the rattle of pool balls. My heart pounded. *What the fuck is he up to now?*

"Let's not forget who's been put in charge tonight, shall we? You owe me this, after all," Roe stammered, his comment to Drip aimed at me—not that he registered that.

"Here. I need to see how many balls that little cunt can handle. And when you're done, I'll let you cum in that tight ass."

Roe stood beside me and pressed his weight against the side of my face, pressure pushing right on the tender spot on my head. He leant in so that we were eye to eye. "Fill you up with every ounce of pressure that he can give you, while I blow a second load all over your face so you can't fucking breath." His eyes were dark—sinister, even.

I darted from one eye to the other, losing myself in the crisp white marking in one of them. He was truly a stunning human, but something inside him had died. It was like the light in his soul had been corrupted. A hint of an impish grin turned his lip, the white hairs on his moustache reminding me that he was still Roe—*kind of.* But it was gone as soon as it appeared.

"And if that doesn't make you black out and think about what you've done, then I'll have Drip make you walk that ass back to your fucking car, so you can fuck off back home."

I nodded, not really sure what else I was able to do or say. I just wanted to cum, so at that point, I'd do anything I had to to get there. I won't lie, the new Roe fucking terrified me more than I'd anticipated he would—and it took a lot for me to actually be terrified by a man. I needed it sometimes, yes, but the situation was...fucked up.

"Aren't you being a little harsh? She said she's learnt her lesson. Can't we just...let her, umm. C-cum?" Mitch asked, regretting the words as they rolled between his lips. *Yes, let me go, or make me cum. I don't give a fuck. Just put me out of my misery.*

"What did you say?" Roe tested.

"N-nothing."

THIRTEEN
Drip

"One...two," Mitch counted with Roe, inserting the coloured resin balls all into Twister's dripping heat. She whimpered and wailed. *Fuck, the sounds coming out of her.* She was so defeated, but Roe was right. I owed it to him, even if it did sound like he was talking to her.

The glossy, wet sound of the balls slowly disappeared through her. Mitch was being so gentle with her. She was so swollen, I couldn't even see her piercing anymore.

"Three. Push it over, make more room," Roe said. Another ball. She was struggling to take it. My jaw tensed. All I wanted was to tell her that she was being such a good girl. She was *begging* for some kind of praise.

"Four."

"Ah! Fuck," she cried out again, the last ball not going all the way in.

Mitch held it in place as Roe took to her mouth with his needy cock, silencing her. He held his hand in a grip around her sweaty tangled hair and pumped into her throat, like she owed him an apology, groaning and hissing through his lips. *Am I missing something? What is his fascination with her to make him act like this?*

I slowed my strokes around my cock to a bare minimum without stopping completely. I needed to calm the fuck down and enjoy the process. But, God, I couldn't fucking wait to blow the load from my balls that was just itching to come out.

"I want you to fuck her ass, nice and slow. Feel the pressure around your cock. When you're ready to cum, I want you to put pressure on the last ball, pushing toward her belly. Got it?" Roe demanded. *What about me? Fuck. How did I go from being the leader to the bottom of the pecking order?*

Twister winced and yelped in both pleasure and pain as Mitch rolled his tongue over her ass. He spat into his hand and rubbed himself, repeating the process until he was covered in saliva. She took him as he pushed in, every hole suddenly penetrated with immense pressure. I could hear the porcelain balls tapping against each other internally, the groans from Mitch and Roe as they fucked her. *Good girl, sis. That's my good fucking girl.*

My cock was vibrating under the grip of my hand, pulsating and dripping with need. It took everything in my body not to scream the praises out to her, but this was her punishment.

"Fuck, I'm going to cum!" Mitch screeched as he pressed against the last ball in Twister's pussy. Muffled screams begged to escape her lips, but Roe's cock was jammed straight into the very back of her throat. *God, me too.* Mitch filled her ass with his pearly white seed as Roe groaned and pounded into her mouth. Webs of his cum dripped from her mouth as he left her.

"Swallow," he commanded. She did, with a cough of defeat. I panted, each breath working hard to feed my brain with oxygen as I tugged myself faster. Ecstasy swam through my head in waves and my balls tightened. I let out a rough groan and heat pooled over my hand before dripping to the carpet.

The heavenly sensation that left my cock eventually subsided, and I could regain my focus. My sister was still on the table panting, crying and quivering. She was going to be sore for a week—no, a month. Mitch put himself away, his cheeks flushed and very well spent. He looked all kinds of fucked up. And still fucking terrified. I didn't blame him. The night had been... there wasn't even a word for the shit that had gone down that whole fucking day.

Roe wiped his leftovers on the table, then pulled a beer from the bar. He threw back the entire bottle as he staggered away, leaving his sweaty notes behind as he disappeared down the hallway. Guilt started to sit on me heavily. Twister needed the release so badly. But, then and there, I would let her suffer. I followed Roe, leaving my sister to her plaything. I needed to grow a pair of balls and be stronger. She might just have learnt her lesson that way. There was no way in hell I could have taught her that lesson. I gave in to her too easily. *I am terribly pussy whipped, so what. I always have been.*

That damn fucking pussy. Heaven.

FOURTEEN
Twister

My phone buzzed for the umpteenth time, but I ignored it.

Again. Drip had been calling me nonstop. If he was that worried about me, he would have shown up. I continued with what I was doing, emptying the tub of fluid into the bucket that I had just bled from Eyeliner in preparation for next month's race. As sore as I was, it needed to be done. I did all my own work with my car. It was the one thing that I could hold onto and enjoy for me; to own it, feel it, claim it and care for it. Nothing else in my life was truly mine.

My body had ached for nearly a week, everything internally and externally had screamed for so long. I was still mad at the fucker. Mad at him for not letting me cum. Mad at him for giving Roe the reins. Mad at him for just fucking standing there with his dick in his hand, and not doing a damn fucking thing about my lack of climax—until I got home. I wasn't sore physically. No, it was a mental comedown. It was fucking exhausting. But I was glad I had Mitch by my side.

I couldn't tell you the psychological feeling I experienced with Mitch that night. He'd untied me, cleaned me, gave me water and food. And then carried me to the bed, where he stayed with me the night. I mean, Drip did that with me too, but this felt...*different*. Drip was my brother. He *had* to love me. But with Mitch, it was a...*a choice*.

My phone vibrated again. *Take a hint—fuck off.* I hit the red button once more. Okay, so I was more than a petty bitch being mad at him for walking out and leaving me without so much as a whisper from him, until then. So many things raced through my head. Everything was fine until Roe came back into the picture.

"Fuck me sideways." I grunted to myself. Rolling my eyes to what was my *shit*uation.

A message lit up on my phone. I rolled my eyes and swiped to open the message.

> **Drip:** If you're going to keep ignoring me, sis, I will have to come over there and show you who's missing you

Three dots showed up on the screen, and then a photo spread across. Tingles shot instantly to my clit at what displayed before my eyes. Drip's hard length, neatly cuddled by his hand with a glossy tip from precum, and thick veins just to prove his point. I squirmed, biting my lip. *For shit's sake*. I wanted him, bad. But I was pissed, so he could get wrecked. *Or maybe I should give him a taste of his own medicine?*

Me: You can take that idea and shove it up your fucking ass, how about that?

"That'll show him. Fucker." I hit send, laughing at my own comment, and then put my phone on my car's wheel on the floor beside me. Thankfully, I had Eyeliner as a distraction. I didn't want to give him the satisfaction of how much I needed him. How much I missed him.

I threaded the bolt back on the reservoir, but the thought of him still barged through my mind, making me pulsate between the thighs.

"No." I deadpanned. *Don't let him get you wet and horny. Don't do it you silly bitch. Don't*—but by the time my brain registered, my fingers had already found my clit. I swirled with a need under my shorts, and then another message dinged once, twice, three times.

"Fuck's sake," I muttered, grabbing my phone again.

> **Drip:** Baby girl, come on. I know you want this. You can't deny me forever

> **Drip:** You're touching yourself aren't you?

> **Drip:** Big brother got that sweet little pussy wet, didn't he?

I didn't reply at first. I was heavily contemplating on if I should, or leave his messages on read and his balls blue. But my head was indeed taken over by the need for him.

> **Me:** Yes…

> **Drip:** Just as I thought. Such a good girl. Talk me through it, sis

I stepped out of my shorts and pulled my greasy shirt off, holding my phone out to take a photo of my hand over my tits. I sat in such a way that he could almost see the top of my pussy, but it was just out of sight. I hit send and he sent back the hot face emoji.

> **Drip:** Why cover?

> **Me:** You think you deserve more?

Drip: I'm so sorry baby. I didn't mean to leave you like that, I had to

Drip: Please, I want to show that pussy how sorry I am

Yeah, that's right, kiss my ass. Fucker. I opened the camera app, making sure the angle was showing my fingers over my piercing. *Hmm, no that's not enough to drive him wild.* I grabbed my new handheld vacuum pump from the bench, opened the seal and put the nozzle into the plastic tube. I sat back down, spread my legs and held the end of the tube over my clit, pumping the handle to create a suction. Immediate waves of heat ran through my veins, and my nipples pinched in an instant.

I held my free arm out for a photo, taking in everything I was doing and nearly hit send– only stopping to hit video call instead. He answered instantly. Or rather, his cock did.

"Jesus fucking hell, girl, you're so wet for me."

He stroked himself, his panty breaths through the speaker as I pumped my sensitive bud until my moans sounded over his.

"Mhmm," I muttered in reply. I pumped a little faster, the sensation of my warm liquid trickling down my ass intensifying my desire.

"Good girl. Show me how you play with it for me," he breathed, matching his pace with mine.

"I think I'm going to...I think I'm going to—" my words fell short as I pressed the red button and the line went dead. A grin pulled my lips ear to ear and a delirious laugh broke from my mouth.

"Don't fuck with me, mother-fucker," I said to myself out loud as I hit aeroplane mode on my phone. I finished myself off with the absolute satisfaction that my brother was probably screaming for me. My climax didn't quite itch the scratch, so I opted for the robotic sex machine that was upstairs in my room.

I fucked myself until it was no longer amusing for me—long past the point of exhaustion, and then rolled myself into a burrito in my blanket and fell into a fitful sleep.

My reflection in the mirror was nothing but amazing, as usual. Clear, olive, youthful skin. Long, wavy chocolate hair that always sat around my face, like I was ready for a grammy award or some shit. The cooling sensation of water as it dripped over my body from the tips of my hair made my skin swarm in goosebumps. I had just gotten out of the shower in preparation for the night's race.

I pulled out my make-up kit, opting for some of my best collections. I didn't *need* any make-up, but I did need to act on the intrusive thought of pissing my brother off just that little bit more.

After hanging up on him and leaving him with blue balls two weeks ago, why not do it again? *If I have the will power, that is.* I threw on a touch of mascara and smudged a little black liner along my bottom lid with my pinky, then pat some hue on my cheeks. I finished the look with a touch of black lipstick by KVD—the only lipstick I had managed to find that wasn't grey or left my lips horribly cracked.

I switched off the hair dryer, flicking my tassels back for the final result.

Hot.

As.

Fuck.

Even I would fuck me. Oh, wait, I do.

Now, time for the fit.

I matched my grungy look with a tight, grey mini skirt, making sure it was my *shortest* one. I opened my lingerie drawer and grabbed my matching red lace set, a garment included in its collection, but hesitated. I bit my lip in thought.

"Hmm. No," I spoke out loud to myself again. I hooked the G-string over my finger, choosing to wear nothing underneath my skirt. I had a plan, of course. I had to pair my outfit with a black lace crop that showed my nipples. Because why the fuck not? I liked it when people looked at me. Besides, we had come this far, I had to send the message loud and clear.

I gave myself one final look in the mirror before checking my phone. Thirteen missed calls and seven messages. *Fuck him. He can wait a little longer.* I needed...*something.* A boost. An orgasm. I quickly ran to my drawer again, grabbing my suction cup toy and slapping it against the tiled wall in the bathroom opposite the mirror, *so I could watch.*

I clutched my tee up over my tits and pinched a nipple, circling the area until it was taut. My heart picked up the pace and worked hard to pump arousal through my veins. My pussy was throbbing for my touch so I backed up closer to the wall, finding a position, and then spread my lips with both fingers and pushed back harder. The cold touch of the wall on my ass sent an electric shock over my skin.

"Oh, shit," I whined as the silicon dildo filled me. Not my favourite toy to play with due to its sheer size, but it was one that I knew would fire me up and get me to squirt on my lingerie—which I now had around my wrist. Nine inches of girth was enough to get me to make a ridiculous amount of mess. I was ovulating too, so the glossy liquid arousal was coming in hot.

I bounced forward and backward over the length to build my climax, swirling my clit with need and squeezing my boob. Watching myself in the mirror only brought it closer. I found the spot where the cock pressed over the knott of my g-spot and swivelled my hips to keep it there, rolling slowly at first, working my speed up as I rolled my fingers over my slippery clit.

"Fuck. Mmhmm," I moaned, panting and swaying. I was close—it was right there. I quickly shook the G-string off my wrist, holding it in a tight ball closer to my pussy, and then began moving my clit horizontally at a much faster pace. Lightning flared over my skin, then to my nipples, my belly button and my pussy and I crashed in a deep shuddering orgasm.

"Ahh," I cried out as the liquid pulsated hard and fast over the fabric, around the cock and down my legs. Whatever the garment failed to soak up puddled on the floor. My body tremored, the sensation of feeling faint striking me for a moment. I gripped the wall with my hands flat and my head as leverage.

"Phew!" I panted. Grabbing my soaked lingerie and sliding off the slick toy, I brushed the fabric over my neck, leaving a wet line over my skin. *This will drive him fucking wild*. I then swiped it over the drenched areas of my pussy, letting it absorb more of the fluid before checking my phone to read the seven messages I ignored earlier.

> **Drip:** Are you coming tonight or what, sis?

Drip: We need you in this race

Drip: Don't do this to me...

Drip: Baby girl, I swear to God

Drip: Reply to me please?

Drip: What do you want? I'll give you anything, I'm sorry. Please

Oh I'm coming alright. You just fucking wait.

I was an hour late by the time I got to the meeting point—by choice, of course. I rolled up right through the centre line of the crowd that had turned up. *Jesus, how many people are here?* I frowned, because what I was seeing was the biggest group yet. *What is the fuss?* I curled my lip for a split second. *Did the fucker not tell me something important?* But then I remembered what was in my hand...a bigger crowd, a bigger reaction.

I scoured for Drip over the last two rows of perfectly parked cars and motorbikes. He was up the back, right in the middle of the string of JDM spec cars, leaning on his R7. I was quick; by the time I got to him I was in a position to circle him. I kept my eyes locked on his grey gaze and dropped down a gear before pushing my foot down on the throttle. In one swift movement I hooked my steering wheel to the left and yanked my handbrake up, turning my wheel to the right.

My rear tyres reacted instantly, screeching and hollering up in smoke as the back end of my car spun out sideways to form a circle around Drip. I held my grip tight on the wheel, not once taking my eyes off him. The sounds of my turbos breathing aggressively to my acceleration and the scent of the burning rubber and unburnt fuel did...*something* to me. I couldn't explain what that sound or smell did to not just my pussy but my *entire* body. I really couldn't.

Drip stood with his arms crossed, inches from my door as I worked perfect circles around him, feathering my foot on the throttle and occasionally pulling the handbrake to maintain my pace. I rolled my tongue over my top teeth, certain that my eyes were smiling for me, and then held my arm out of the window, my G-string hanging by my finger. He took it and his eyes widened, no doubt feeling how wet they were before narrowing his glare. I circled him one more time before leaving him in a cloud of smoke and driving off. I could see him sniffing my lingerie through my rearview mirror before he tucked them away in his jeans.

I found another group I was familiar with and parked Eyeliner up beside them. More and more people started to roll in and mingle. More expensive cars showed and more money was being handed around between everyone, hundreds and thousands—if not millions of dollars' worth of bets being made.

How fucking exhilarating.

FIFTEEN
Drip

Sometimes I forgot that she was my sister—well, she wasn't. *But she was,* in a fucked up kind of way.

How long is this going to keep going? The back and forth and back again, like real siblings do, but like a fucking married couple?

Twister and I bickered more than I ever had with my own fucking twin—*bite me and I'll bite back harder*—always revenge plotting each other.

But I knew the second she circled me into her smokey haze drift, and dropped her soaked lingerie in my hand that I was not the one in control.

She was.

And always would be.

I'd be the first to admit that I had overstepped the boundary—a little. But I wanted to see how far Roe would take her. Was I guilty that he had taken it too far? Yes. But did the smell of the little red lace G-string that was marinated in her cum make me forget it all entirely? Yes. She was fucking pissed. And insanely hot. But I wasn't done with her—*yet. A whole hour past schedule? To our biggest race yet?*

I looked her up and down, and my jaw tensed. *Fuck.* She was dolled up to the fucking nines and her hair looked like she had fucked herself senseless—which would explain the wet patch that was filling my back pocket. My dick twitched. She was fucking glorious, like a whole ass meal that was just begging to be eaten. And I would not hesitate to devour every last drop of her, not leaving a single fucking crumb for Satan himself. She flirted with her eyes as I lowered mine, mindlessly gnawing on my lips at the sight of the woman. All of her skin showed through the lace, her boobs making the fabric strain, nipples out and all, on display for all to see—like my cock was about to be if she looked at me like that again.

What's the bet the minx isn't wearing anything under that short skirt either?

Fuck. That skirt.

Twister was aiming high, leaving only imagination to do the rest of the work of what awaited under the fabric that clung to her tight little body. Her striped slate skirt hung high on her hips in a way that made a lump form in my throat. Her lips were stained in a shade of black that I had not seen her wear since forever, and behind the smudged layer of makeup was a glint in her eye that I needed to fuck out.

She gasped from the blow of air leaving her chest as I pinned her against the door of her car by her frail little neck.

"You better give me a good fucking reason as to why you're late," I growled as her jugular pulsated under my thumb. It was probably a little too strong, but she knew just how to get under my skin, and I was hard and vexed. Plus, there was a lot of money at stake.

A rumble of laughter simmered in her chest, so I leant my weight onto her. My erection pressed hard against her thigh, showing her what she did to me. A whimper slithered through her lips as mine hovered only inches from hers. I inhaled, losing my senses for a second, and then drew in another breath until I was dizzy. *What in the fuck is that smell on her neck?* It was sweet, and something else I couldn't put a name to. *Wait. Is that...her cum? Did she bathe herself in it or some shit?*

I groaned and she shuddered from my hot breath shooting down her spine. Her body grew tense, I knew she was fighting for her life trying to stay mad at me but I could tell there was just no fucking way she could control that mind of hers. *Minx. Fucking minx.*

"You better not fuck this up for me tonight, sis," I demanded with a corrupt grin. Little did she know, I was going to make winning this race very fucking hard for her.

She smacked her lips together. "Fuck. You," she whispered before shoving her elbow against my chest, breaking contact from her neck and ducking under my grip. I laughed as she took two steps away and yanked her tiny physique backwards, before I slammed her against the car and drew her hands behind her back. *I've had enough of this fucking merry-go-round.*

She struggled but failed against my strength, eventually accepting defeat as I pressed her face over the bonnet, her breath fogging over the steel. I spread her knees apart with mine and leant into her ear.

"You will, baby girl. You fucking will."

SIXTEEN

Twister

If I could spit in his face, I would. But the repercussions weren't worth the energy.

Plus, I had my cheek squashed flat on the bonnet of my car. I'd already dug myself a big enough hole, I didn't need to keep digging. *It's worth it though, he is up to something and I know it's going to be deliciously painful...for me.*

"Nope. My pussy is closed. So sorry," I objected playfully. I was absolutely not fucking him. He could stew in that thought. I squirmed as his free hand planted on me, setting my skin alight with the back of his hand as he trailed it upward. *No, push the thought out. Don't give in to him.*

"Naughty girl, you shouldn't need any more reminders." His words rolled off his tongue and through my veins like a drug. Drip was back to his normal self again, not like he was that night.

Possessive.

Controlling.

And needy.

"Reminders of what, exactly?" I humoured him. As much as I tried to hide it, my tone was too low and broken. I couldn't help it. I needed him. Always. And not the Drip that he was around Roe. I needed *my* Drip. My brother. He hesitated his response, the air between us cracking.

"You know the answer to that. So are you going to be a good girl or not?"

"That depends."

"On what, sis?"

"On if you're going to leave me like that again. You know how much—" I weakened, but he cut me off.

"You deserved it." He slid his hand over my ass and gripped my hip, then jolted my ass against his erection again. "Now. I'm going to ask again," he growled. The sensation of his hot breath in my ear buzzed to my clit, making my mouth water.

I gasped as something cool and firm trailed up my leg, stopping at the arc of my thigh. I mindlessly tried to close my legs but he held them spread with his. He slowly pressed it into my now-wet slit.

"Jesus fucking hell." I blew out a whine. *The pressure.* I held in a breath and furrowed my brows to focus on the object that was *very* deep inside me. My head fuzzed as everything swelled to accommodate its length. It was smooth, like acrylic or resin maybe. It was thick and very long, and I could feel that it was cylinder-shaped. *Whatever the fuck it is, I am in for a treat...punishment.*

Drip stopped pushing when he felt resistance. I gagged involuntarily to the immense constraint, and then he pushed it a little further. *Oh, hell.*

"Are you going to be *my* good girl?" His words were merely a whispered moan. At that point, I was completely speechless, breathless, feeling my pussy clench around what I assumed was his car's shifter. He withdrew his fingers, leaving the object inside me and tenderly rubbed my ass. I opened my mouth to say something—*anything*. But nothing but air and whimpers left my lips. My pussy pulsated again as he played with my hair, taking a section of it around his hand. He grumbled something I didn't fully register, and then he tilted my head back enough so that whatever was in my pussy hit the brink of my inner wall again from the pressure of his thigh. *I'm about to crumble for him here and now.*

"You didn't answer my question. You speak when spoken to, do you understand?"

"Mhmm," was all I could mutter out. His fingers found my clit and worked me tightly.

"Words, baby."

"Yes, I will be your good girl," I moaned my defeat, then he spun me around to face him with such speed I got whiplash.

Without warning, he stole my air with a kiss, keeping my head prisoner to his hand as it held the nape of my neck. His taste liquified my legs entirely.

"You're going to be my good girl and win the race for your brother...with this inside you, aren't you?"

"Yes," I answered with as much truth as I could possess.

"And what are you going to do after you win for me?"

"I don't —" I hadn't a clue what he wanted me to do.

"You're going to wait at the finish line for me. I want you face down and your ass up on that fucking bonnet. Am I understood, sis?"

"Yes." *Jesus fucking Christ, can we do it now?*

"Good. Now, go win me that race. If you can manage to do it without passing out."

I took *one* step forward as Drip walked off and the object between my legs took my breath away. It twitched, and rolled and...vibrated? "Oh, fuck," I muttered to myself. It was better than any dildo. *What in the actual fuck is he doing to me?* Every theory made me doubt that it was a shifter. The vibration felt like kegel balls, but the shape was almost identical to the gear shifter he had in his car, and the one I used in mine.

This is going to be a long—painful night.

A familiar-sounding engine rolled closer. The exact same car as mine, only in bright pink. A Nissan Skyline GTR R35. It stopped and two bright pink high-heeled shoes with straps up to the knees came from under the suicide door and then a drop-dead bombshell of a woman followed. My rival for tonight—and the first woman to *ever* race me.

She was tall and slender, tits a bare handful but an ass you could see from the side. Peroxide blonde hair, with tones of brown and black underneath. *Mmm, yummy.*

"Twister?" She smiled, swaying towards me. She held out her hand and I shook it. *What am I, famous?* "It's an honour."

"What's your name, pretty?" I flirted, unable to ignore the constant humming in my pussy.

"Ivy."

"Nice car, Ivy."

"Thanks. It's inspired by you."

"I can see that. Right down to the little number plate on display in your window—'warped.' But I already own a nice GTR. I don't need another one," I threatened, just slightly.

"What makes you think you're going to win?" Ivy added, matching my energy. Which made me squirm with delight and arousal.

"I don't *think*. *I know*," I snickered. *Now I know this is why the race is so popular tonight. Girl on girl.* The truth was, I didn't need any more cars. But I bet that pussy tasted like fucking mangoes. "Are you aware of the rules of this race, Ivy?"

"I assume so?" She questioned in barely a breath.

"Okay. Tell me, have you been with a woman before?"

"What?" Her cheeks flushed in an instant, those once pale cheeks showing all of her innocence. She was like a female version of Mitch. And didn't that make things more...interesting? I knew she was going to be fun to play with.

I stepped forward with everything that I could, squeezing my thighs together and stepping into her little bubble that she clearly melted under. I was slightly taller than her, which worked in my favour. I tenderly brushed her chin with my thumb, and she reacted immediately with a gaspy inhale.

"Have you been with a woman, Ivy?" I asked her slower than the last, and as though no one was around us. But that just simply wasn't true. I smirked insincerely, turning around to let her eyes wander over everyone. She swallowed and looked back at me, then looked at Drip. He was standing next to Roe, who hadn't taken his hungry eyes off Ivy.

"But what if I win?"

"Either way, I still get to fuck you, Ivy." I was so fucking turned on.

"What about...him?" She squeaked, turning her gaze back to Drip. "He's hot as fuck. Is he—your boyfriend?"

"My brother," I corrected her with a flared nose. A strange sensation made its course through my veins, like anger, but not.

"Oh, even better. I can take him too then."

I laughed, and she joined in as if she knew why I began laughing in the first place. *Okay, I'll entertain the thought. But touch him and I'll rip your clit from between your legs and make you fucking eat it.*

SEVENTEEN

Drip

OBEDIENT. O-FUCKING-BEDIENT LITTLE MINX, I groaned to myself as I stared right down the firing line of my sister's pink pussy—and her opponent's. Twister was shining like a diamond under that mini skirt, the tender skin of her labia very clearly struggling to hold the clear rod I had shoved in there earlier. Even from a distance, I could see that she was tight...and so fucking swollen, thigh to thigh with her opponent, Ivy, who was proudly as eager to play our twisted little games. *That's my good girl.*

Holy. Damn. My balls throbbed. Ivy's pink G-string was hung by the stem of her high-heeled shoe. *Two women? Do I get two holes to fuck right now? Or is Twister just choking my chain?* I couldn't be certain if this was just getting back at me, but I'd roll with it. *Fuck, I wish Roe was here to see this.* He was on babysitting duties tonight, keeping our Mitchy boy company.

Twister's scent was still intoxicating my brain, and I hadn't stopped inhaling the secretions from her lingerie. I was drunk...on her.

The fog lights from the two cars beside them set the scene, a delicious combination of shadows and light on both of the beauties. Twister and Ivy had their faces pressed against the bonnet of Twister's car and their asses' pointing up to the sky above us, just like I had asked her.

My stomach swirled. I'd not been with *two* women before. It had always just been me and Twister. All of our rivals had been men since we first started The Underground. All the more reason to assume that she was up to no good after not having sent this girl on her merry way. Perhaps shoving my car's shifter in her pussy made her think straight?

Twister wasn't the jealous type—I didn't think so, anyway. How could she be? She loved being shared. I guess she was the one being shared...not me. But she was unpredictable. She wouldn't hesitate to put a bitch in her place if they ever tried to get with me. Even a sly glance from Ivy earlier and she was barking like a fucking dog. She was a fucking lunatic, but I loved her. We could never really be a thing, not really. We didn't need to be. Pretending to be her boyfriend in public was probably as close as we would ever get to 'dating'.

You don't date your sister.

Well, you don't fuck them either. And sisters certainly don't get on their knees with their asses in the air with a dripping wet pussy that's just begging to be destroyed...bringing a new friend along for the ride too.

I adjusted myself, coming to my senses that my jeans had become taut. My cock was very solid and itching to be submerged into something wet, and tight.

"So fucking obedient, sis. And you've convinced a new plaything into our game," I said as I stroked my index finger along the base of Ivy's ankle, dragging it upwards slowly. She whimpered softly and wiggled her ass, but stayed in her position. *What a sensitive, eager little thing.* "What good girls."

I walked back to the other side of the car towards Twister. "Now. Who gets me first?" I added.

Twister cracked a small laugh under her breath. *I fucking knew it, she's definitely up to something.*

My heart pounded for only a brief second because I heard my car—that I did not bring tonight. It was humming, roaring from a distance, closing in at great speeds. It wasn't long before it was parked alongside Twister's car. Roe stumbled out, dressed in grey track pants and a tight black shirt.

"I heard the word pussy, in segments of two. So I came running," he said as he threw one of my spare shifters towards me. I caught it and huffed under my breath with a turned smile. "You're lucky I had a spare one lying around." He winked. The bulge in his pants was adamant that Twister absolutely had something planned. *Cheeky fucking bitch.* I was only slightly disappointed that I wasn't getting two girls, but at least I had Twister to myself.

"You're supposed to be...babysitting,"

Roe slapped his palm over my shoulder, but I didn't move an inch considering the strength he had put into it. "Don't worry yourself, boss. I made sure he was good and snug." He winked and turned his attention to the girls. He rolled his tongue over his lips and rubbed his hands together. "Now, let's not keep these delicious, patiently waiting pussies like that for too long. They need some caressing. And earning all this money makes us men so...*hungry*," Roe growled the last part of the sentence as he eyed off his next target—Ivy. His predatory glare enticed everything inside me to spark and crack with energy.

An inaudible sound slipped from Twister's lips as I planted my hand over the line where her ass and thigh connected, then pinched the tender skin before helping her up off the bonnet.

"Come, sis." I demanded.

I sat in the driver's seat of my Supra and rolled the seat as far back as I could. I tapped my thigh and Twister spread out on top of me, her flushed, tired face concentrating hard on keeping her little token inside of her like I had asked. "Good girl," I praised, tugging back the loose strays of hair that covered her face behind her ear. The sweet smell of her heat was quick to hit my nose again and my cock reacted, pumping heavily against the taut seams.

My breath hitched, seeing her bright eyes filled with such need and desperation for me. I knew she couldn't hold out—not with the shifter in her. I had it made of glass for her, with kegel balls scattered inside it. *Every turn, every bump, every slide*. Every time she pulled that handbrake for another corner it would have sent her fucking wild, right near the edge of climax but just out of reach. It was a miracle she even won the race, but she was *my* Twister.

She did not lose.

Ever.

Her chest worked hard to collect air as she sat on my lap, panting but unable to speak a word. She planted her hand on my chest and her lips moved, with no sound at first.

"I-I...I need..." Her voice was low, broken and shaky. She was fucking exhausted. Had I taken it too far? The burn of her needy breath rolled over my skin. I grabbed her cheeks to force her eyes to mine. Her makeup was smudged from sweat. I narrowed my brows.

"You need what?"

She croaked another nothing, her mouth still moving but no sound following. Her skin was burning up under my palms and her nipples pinched tight. Twister's body was aching and screaming for me... if only she could just say it.

"Are you swollen for me, sis?"

"Mhmm."

"Do you want me?" I spoke softly as I trailed my hand down her chest, tucking my fingers under and pulling the fabric of her top over the top of her boobs.

"Y-Yes."

"Then tell me." I squeezed her nipple firmly, the way she liked it and then kept her balance with my hands at the small of her back. It took her a second to pull herself together to form more than a one-syllable word. She looked totally tongue-tied, dazed and drunk. Having the shifter inside her for so long had clearly made her ability to think fall short.

"I want you."

"Show me where, baby. Where do you want me?" I rocked her into my lap a little further, pressing my cock against the hard object between her thighs and her red cheeks blossomed more. The pressure caused her mouth to form an O, sucking all the air into her chest, but none coming back out. I groaned. *I can't wait to fill my cum in that beautiful fucking mouth.*

Her tiny hand reached back for mine and struggled as she directed it to the soft spot of her inner thigh. I felt an immense amount of pleasure just from her touch as the soft spot of my fingers trailed her soft skin. Goosebumps formed over her body as she led my touch to where the intense heat was radiating from.

"Here," she squeaked desperately in merely a breath. *Fuck.* I loved it when she did that, fully losing herself for me, begging, submitting to me. The sassy side of her was long gone, it was just her vulnerable side and me now.

I made contact with the sensitive wet bud with my thumb. On impact, she cooed and rolled her neck so far back that the ends of her silky hair tickled my other hand. I fought every urge in my body. I wanted to annihilate that tight little hole right then and there, claim her, own her, worship her and fill her with my love until she had no more room left. But slow and steady would win this race.

I could feel the resin toy pulsating, pushing out slightly before retreating back in again with each pulse of her pussy. "Please." She added.

I pushed my fingers around the shifter, she winced as her pussy clenched down around me. I drew in a sharp breath, her arousal trickled down my hand, coating it in her clear heat. My cock pounded aggressively against the seam of my jeans, begging to be free, begging for a release.

I pushed the shifter in a little further until I felt resistance, making sure to press it on a slight angle towards her belly—the knot of pressure. She swallowed, pulsated and then moaned deeply with a shivering breath.

"Good girl. You can take it," I pushed it harder again, receiving the same reaction, and then pulled it out slowly, leaving her hollow and empty with desperation. She blinked and furrowed her brows...like I had just removed the venom from a snake bite and she was coming to her senses once more. We both looked down at the glass shifter as she caught her breath. It was filled with glitter, skull-shaped kegel balls and a small strip of neon lights that illuminated when connected to the gearstick. The tip was also mostly glitter, so it sparkled like a disco ball.

"So wet, little minx. For me?"

"Mhmm," she mumbled. I planted the glass gently at the base of her bottom lip. "No. Use your words with me, please."

She inhaled through her nose heavily drawing in her scent before exhaling a shuddering moan.

"Yes, for you."

"For *who?*" I pressed for an answer, nudging the stick a little firmer so her bottom teeth were fully exposed.

"My brother," she whispered.

"That's my good twisted little sister. Clean," I demanded. Her eyes rolled into the back of her head and then she tilted her head back with her mouth wide open. "Such a good girl. Mmm, so fucking good."

I rewarded her with my words as the lengthy wet cylinder slid over the flat of her tongue. A thoughtless groan slipped from my lips and she whimpered, both of us now toying on the very edge of our limits. We were both a little *too good* at foreplay and edging, what with all those years of practice and all. But she wouldn't win with me—*not tonight.*

She swirled her tongue around it, her cheeks dipping inwards as I fed it out and then swelling again when I pushed it back in her mouth. She cleaned every inch of her liquid up, swallowing, drooling and moaning to her own flavours.

"Describe your taste for me," I breathed as I removed it from her mouth to speak. She gulped, then licked the leftovers from her lips. I let her slowly find her words through her panting.

"Umh. Sweet, but kind of metallic? And...velvety."

"Yes, good. Now tell me, what was it that you wanted again?" I asked playfully, leaning over to twist the glass shifter onto my gear stick. She leant into my chest and wrapped her arms around my neck, panting into my ear, soft like butter and entirely mine for the taking.

Sometimes I wasn't just her brother—I was her fuck buddy, where she would want nothing but to be used and abused, hit and destroyed, her hair pulled and her skin left raw from whatever landed across it. I was her fantasy. Whatever she asked me to do I did, to fulfil her needs and desires. Because I loved her. She was fucking wild. She had asked me to her pussy once, she had said it had to be while she was unconscious.

I did it. *Of course I did*. I would do *anything* for her.

Her pussy was branded in *my* name.

D.

R.

I.

P.

Tattooing her while she was unconscious wasn't the worst part. It was the fucking chloroform to get her unconscious. Sometimes I didn't think I possessed the capabilities to accommodate her in all the twisted ways that she wanted me—the ways she *needed* me. *But I try. I try so fucking hard for her.*

And then, sometimes, I *was* her brother. To be there for her, when all she wanted was someone to hold her. To rub her feet when we watched chickflick movies. To tell her everything would be okay. To free her mind, her body, her soul and her spirit. To wash, brush and plait her hair. To dote on and love on her.

To feel needed.

Wanted.

Like an abandoned, wounded, homeless little girl truly deserved.

My heart sank to the pit of my stomach at the memory.

"You, Drip." Her broken little pleads only tapped at the soft spot in my heart. I knew she only wanted me, then and there, but I wanted to see how good that shifter could make her cum...*the way her little fuck machine did, all those weeks ago.*

Little minx, trying to tease me with a video call and then leave me with aching balls, like I wasn't watching her. Little did she know I had cameras set up everywhere in her room.

I had since she was sixteen. Not for the reason people would assume. I wasn't a creep... back then. I genuinely needed to keep an eye on her because of self-harm. I was obsessed with her, with keeping her safe. How else could I protect her from herself? She was dangerous, and I refused to lose her. Like I said, I loved my sister in every possible way.

I looked out my window and jolted my head at Roe, who was going to town in Ivy's ass. *Rough. So rough.*

"Come over here baby," I commanded, lifting Twister's ass up slightly and hovering her over to the centre of my car. She followed my instructions and found her balance with one foot on my seat next to my leg, and the other on the passenger seat. She was off in her own world, absent-minded and needing all of me to control her every move.

"I want you to fuck the shifter first. Do you think you can do that for me?" I ran my hand down her back and kissed a part of her neck that seemed to always disable a part of her brain.

"Okay," she whimpered.

"Atta girl. I want to see how you can make yourself cum on it like you did in your bathroom tonight, and with that little machine in your room."

"What?"

"Shh. That's not important right now. Sit, baby," I demanded, the need in my cock weighing heavily on my arousal for her. She nodded and stretched backward, using her elbows on the dash to hold her up as she lowered herself onto the shifter.

"Ah," she gasped for air and inhaled sharply between her teeth.

"That's it, Twister. Fuck my shifter like my cock."

EIGHTEEN

Twister

Fucking hell this man. I mean, kegel balls? Really? Well, I guess they worked, didn't they? I was completely and utterly hypnotised. I had no reins of control anymore. I just wanted him to take me.

Claim me. Fill me with his need. *And his...seed. No—I can't do that again. I won't.* But I wanted to. *If I could just use my fucking words...god damn it!* My brother and the ways he could get under my skin. *Jesus. Has he not tortured me enough?*

I desperately wanted his possessive, webbed heat to flow straight into me. I wanted him to fill me so much that he could smell himself seeping from my pores. Marking his territory. It was so wrong, but I didn't care anymore.

I wanted to be back on his lap more than anything, but I just *had* to sit on this thing first. The coolness from the shifter quickly warmed inside me as I lowered myself over the glass toy. I fell away in my thoughts and sensations, barely able to focus on Drip's words as he told me to make myself cum. Which was painfully close. But that was the thing about orgasm control *and denial*...it took fucking ages to bring it back again.

It took everything out of me to use my legs as balance as I lifted and lowered slowly over the glass. In the very corner of my eye, I saw Roe and Ivy. They had moved from the bonnet of my car to the back seat. A smile turned my lips for a split second. I knew he couldn't resist a woman like that. I wanted Drip to myself. All I had to do was send Roe a photo of her ass and he was screeching down the road in minutes. Besides, there was no way I was sharing my brother in our current predicament—this was between me and him.

If I could manage to keep Roe busy, then I could have my brother back...the way he was. I still wanted Roe and the way he made me feel. But not then. And then there was Mitch. *Fuck...Mitch. What happened, is he okay?* I hadn't heard from in...weeks. *Fuck.*

I felt the sensation of dizziness run through my head. I couldn't focus anymore, the pulsating need in my pussy hurting so much that it was tightening my stomach. But I maintained a steady rhythm, my climax building the more I stretched to my fullest, lifting and lowering myself over the shifter.

The very thing that had spent the last few hours in my body.

Hounding me for a release.

I'm close, so very close.

But Drip just had to up it a notch, didn't he? He turned the key and the engine began to rumble to life. "Oh. God," I panted from the vibration of the shifter rattling inside me.

"Yes, , cum for me. Cum for your brother." His voice broke slightly, showing its coarse rough edge through his desperate plea. "Ah!"

My body tensed as I clenched over the solid glass. A lightning pinch cracked in the low of my belly and ricocheted into my climax, releasing a steady stream of liquid down the stick that collected into a puddle on the leather. I shuddered and panted from the intensity, my head spinning from the release and my legs quivering and struggling to hold me up.

Drip grabbed me, pulling me off the stick, and sat me on his lap once more. He pushed me backward slightly and filled me with his thickened hunger, not once giving me a chance of a breath as he pumped into me.

Deep.

Hard. So hard.

I struggled to accommodate him. He was harder than he had ever been before, and he had me straddled with total possession. The tips of his fingers dug into my ass and his thumbs were firmly pressed into the arc of my hip bones as he used them to control my hips.

He adjusted his hand and moved his digit over the metal bar of my clit, swirling with need and sending me into another climax.

"I'm—ahh." I couldn't get the words out, the severity of pressure silencing my every thought, every word.

"Fuck, yes, baby," he purred breathlessly. He was building his own orgasm, pounding into me through the pulsing clenches of mine. The torment of swelling from having the shifter in me for so long created a resistance of pressure in my pussy. The sounds of our juices collided between us, clacking with each thrust as we fucked our stupid love song to bed.

My climax finally deprecated and I could use my head again. *I think?*

"I want you to fill me," I begged.

"What?" He sounded like he was in autopilot, short-circuiting from my wetness.

"I want you to cum inside me, please."

"What happened last time, T?" His voice was suddenly stern and in full control, yet seemingly disappointed in my demand.

"Fuck last time. Just do it, please," I begged, a tear of desperation forming under the lid of my eye but not yet falling. I pivoted my hips to take him even deeper again until I almost gagged from the pressure, and in turn, the warm droplet crawled down my cheek.

"Fuck." He winced, pulling me closer and stealing a kiss from me before sucking my tit into his mouth.

He thrust deeper and harder into me with a second or two between each one, like he hated to hurt me and loved it in unison. I had wanted him to cum in me since the last time I felt it happen. There was truly no better sensation than being filled like that.

But that was with Phantom, not Drip.

I couldn't tell Drip. I wouldn't. My secrets *had* to stay in the tomb that was my fucking soul.

I couldn't have gone to a fucking doctor. He would have found out who's it was in some way or another. I couldn't tell *anyone*. I was alone. What a fucking mess. How would Drip still love me if I told him that I killed his brother, let alone was carrying his bastard child? I had to take matters into my own hands. *I did it myself.*

Drip had found me in the bathroom.

Unconscious.

Covered in thick crimson.

Naked.

With a bleach bottle sitting beside me around a row of needles and an old coat hanger on the floor. He hadn't told me anything else about what happened other than how terrified he was of losing me. I was all he had left.

Both he *and* I hadn't been the same since. It completely destroyed Drip seeing me that way. He hadn't let me from his sight since, even going as far as setting up cameras and wiring my phone. Watching me everywhere I went, everything I did. Every*one* I did.

"I'm going to cum, Twister. Cum with me." Drip circled at my clit again and spiralled me into another climax. "Yes, that's it."

I pulsated around him through my orgasm and felt an absence for a second before a warm wave of his cum threaded over my clit. Intensifying the fireworks in my pussy even further. "Good girl. Good girl."

"Oh, fucking hell, Drip," I squalled. But I needed more. I knew he wouldn't cum in me, not without having a vasectomy. One day my brother will own me, in the same way I owned him.

Savagely.

NINETEEN
Drip

"Where did you find this one?" Roe laughed, shaking his head. He was observing everything before him and looked in total disbelief, yet somewhat satisfied with how we got here. It had been six months having him back home.

The Underground wasn't the same without him, and it was even better now than it was before he left us. I studied the man before me as he began pacing around Twister's car with his arms crossed, seeing the slight swell of his cock in its wake. He was far from what he was seven years ago. As was I, very much so. I could see the different shades of his patched skin showing through the ink that overlapped them. Despite his efforts in trying to hide his skin condition with tattoos, the white patches that coated his body had spread since he'd been in jail. There were even ones I hadn't noticed behind the glass screen when I visited him. But his persona there was different to now.

138

I chuckled, furrowing my brow and matching his disbelief. Where did we find him? *We didn't. That's the best part.*

"He...found *us*," I spoke proudly. We were pretty lucky to score Mitch, actually. I had to admit, I'd grown quite fond of the kid. He was loyal and eager to please. Not just me, but either one of us. He was a great fit for my club. He was there when I needed him. He dropped anything at my demand and was by my side where I needed him—or if *she* needed him. If I needed eyes on the city, he was there. If I needed eyes around the track, he was there. If I needed a lead out to keep cops off my ass, he was there.

Shit he would kiss the ground if I fucking asked him. Where would I be without him? I didn't know, he was just...good like that. He just did things which gave me more time to do other shit. He even took over dealing with my imports and exports internationally. That was where the big money was.

My eyes stayed pinned on Twister, who was gnawing on her bottom lip in ecstasy as Mitch's tongue lapped up her and Roe's liquid, which had spread like butter over the delicate areas of her pussy. Until every drip was gone. Only to have more trail down the seam of her swollen hole and down to her back door before collecting on the bonnet. Her favourite spot. And ours, it seemed.

Mitch's teeth nibbled at her clit piercing, as he always did. Though I couldn't be sure if doing it was *her* aphrodisiac or *his*.

He swallowed again, uncertain if it was cum or blood he was swallowing this time.

"Fucking hell, you two. Mmm," I groaned in joy as I adjusted myself, releasing some of the pressure. I could watch them two all day, every day and never get tired of it. *Well, I do anyway.* She squirmed underneath him with a needy deep moan. He was nearly sending her off the edge again.

I don't know why we hadn't done it sooner—breed her.

Breeding.

My sister.

Seeing her eyes roll into the back of her head while someone filled her up like a fucking jam donut was euphoric. And the noises. *The fucking noises.* I would kill to have her feel that any time she wanted it.

"God damn, I could get used to this. What about you big boy?"

"Count me in. I love anyone who drinks my cum like a glass of water. Take it from me." Roe winked and lit up a cigarette, moving to sit himself on the roof of the car and watch as the heated fuckery before us only continued to unfold. The cunt was fucking wild. What even was my life? Sick and fucking twisted. But did I give one single shit?

Absolutely the fuck not.

It was getting harder to ignore the throb in my cock, but I couldn't look away. *Don't cum, don't cum, don't cum—it will hurt! I know it will.* I winced at the thought. *"Don't orgasm until you are healed."* The famous last words from the Dr. ran through my brain on repeat. However long ago that was.

Drink his cum like a glass of water. Well, yeah Mitch was. I shouldn't be surprised, he had drunk mine when we first met. And even after Roe and I kept the damn kid locked up in one of my estates for a month—*a whole fucking month*—he still chose to stay with us. He was one of us now, and it has been a helluva six months.

I knew I'd never have Roe back to where he was before jail. But that feeling I had with him, was almost like I had my brother back again—*my real brother.* I couldn't explain it to save my life, but seeing Twister lying on the bonnet of her magenta-coloured car, fully submitted to her surroundings, coated in a thick layer of sweat, and in a puddle of Roe's cum did something to my brain that it really shouldn't.

I had spent the last ten years scratching my head, over and over again, repeating the same fucking bullshit. Torturing myself for answers that I never found...and would never find. Growling at myself that I was sick. Sick and pathetic. Just not made for this earth for the things that I did to my sister after that night I found her on the bathroom floor.

My sister.

Ten.

Fucking.

Years.

After a while, those questions depleted. Because I loved her. Had I recovered after losing a part of me? No. Could I ever? Probably not. I'd been with Phantom since we were tadpoles in Dad's balls, peas in the pod, you know? And Twister had been with us since we were kids, after finding her sleeping in our school's gym one morning. She wasn't a student at our school. She was cold, wet, and dirty, with cuts and bruises all over. She had no home to go back to.

Phantom and I decided to keep her, as if she was a lost puppy or some shit. We kept her hidden in my parents' granny flat at the back of our family home in the suburbs. But they eventually found out. It wasn't exactly easy to hide a rebellious energetic kid in your house with a blabbering twin brother talking about a new sister all the time. But after all that, she just became...*our sister*. That was our new life. Twister was always...*different*. Her mind was so beautifully broken, and lethal. A damaged soul, like mine came to be.

But how many times have you fucked your sister? Does it mess with your head too? It did with mine. Running The Underground and riding my R7 was sometimes my only clarity. And tattoos. Barely an inch of my skin was left that wasn't coated in black ink. Other than my face, which was *hard* off limits. It was the one thing that I had left of my brother. *My reflection.* My eyes were a glass mirror of his. Tattoos had always stopped the pain of losing my brother, and equally punished me for what I did with my sister.

I was always needing to feel something that wasn't fully submerged in the thoughts of fucking her. And it all started when she was sixteen...when we let her have boys over. I would always find myself needing...needing to listen to her. Listening to how her body reacted and changed for her partners of choice. Listening to her make herself cum. *For two whole years.* And then watching her, which I was certain she knew about. Then those feelings became stronger, and stronger. And then it all changed.

Seven years ago, I discovered something about myself that I really should have stayed curious about. I wasn't the only twisted one in our family who was thinking those things—she was too.

My twisted sister.

And now all I lived for was to feel her, and only her. Every emotion I had, was for her. Every decision I made, was for her. Every part of my being, was hers.

"Twisted, isn't he?" Roe's raspy *smoked-too-many-cigarettes-in-jail* voice broke my train of thought. I shook my head, coming back to the reality before me. "Just like us," I added. Because he was.

Mitch was licking his own fucking cum from Twister. He had already blown his load in her, while I was too busy in my own little mindless thoughts. *For fuck's sake, why do I have to drift off at the wrong bloody moments?* I laughed again, pure joy seeping from my chest, and Roe had the audacity to look at me like I was some crazy person. Like reality was only just becoming apparent with me.

"Yep. This is *our* life mate. Fucking hell," I said in disbelief.

"This...this is our life," he repeated as his arms swung wide open, stepping back and gesturing to the cars that surrounded us, then to his softened dick before waving to Mitch and Twister.

"Ah, if only *he* could see us now." I thought I owned this city with Phantom before, but the power I had now was far greater. Would he have fucked Twister if he was alive? Would he have been into...*this?* God damn, just the thought of us tag-teaming her made me want to cum there and then. I adjusted myself again, the pulsation hounding me heavily. I needed to cum. *But would he, though...if he was alive?* Maybe not. He was prissy like that.

I may not have my brother, but I did own the whole fucking city—something *he* wanted. Everyone respected me. I was fucking king. *Phantom could have been king right here with me.* Especially now that I had a bigger crew. More eyes around the streets. My city.

Our city.

Business was great. Higher-end cars were on offer, with bigger buy-ins, and tougher competition. We shot them in the foot, each and every fucking time. Funny how many people throw a wad of cash for a taste of my sister...or girlfriend, as they so thought.

"If only," Roe mirrored my words sarcastically. His tone was slow and almost domineering...*questionable*. I frowned, because I couldn't quite put the feeling to words. Like he knew something I didn't.

Mitch tucked himself away and put his shirt back on. He ran his hand through his sweaty curls and staggered back to the bike I bought for him. He would be ready for his first race soon. But if he was going to start racing for me, I was going to need someone to take his place. He brought in a lot of strays for me, ones who had money to burn. Which in turn kept my Twister happy.

One dick just wasn't enough for her. *What did I do to deserve such a woman?* It was every man's fucking dream to have the control over who she fucked. And yet, she was so loyal to me, never once going behind my back to get her pussy wet. It was always by my command. Even if they didn't want to fuck her back. I couldn't tell you how good it felt when I made someone fuck my sister when they didn't want to. Forcing someone to shove their weapon in her hole. It did something to me. I didn't know what, but it was something.

"How are your balls holding up? Ready to blow a load yet or what?" Roe sneered, once again pulling my attention back to the now. I'll admit it was fucking hard to watch them breed her without the ability to do it myself. I was still healing after all…from the surgery that I had been putting off *for far too long*.

"Doc said two weeks," I declared, unable to hide the desperation in my voice for my need of release. Roe had come with me when I got my vasectomy—*how ever the fuck long ago that was.* It felt like a fucking century ago the last time I climaxed, and I couldn't wait to do it inside my sister.

Roe had tuned into my idea of breeding her and he was all in. No questions asked.

Did we make a breeding pact?

Yes. Yes we did. Roe had a vasectomy the week before Mitch did. Now that was fucking commitment. Of course, in rotation, for my sister's sake. Had to keep her fed, at all costs.

"It's been three, Drip."

"Oh, shit."

TWENTY
Twister

How much cum can that pussy handle, sis?

Now that was a question I didn't have the answer to. And it was going to take me a damn fucking hot minute to buffer. *Can you give me about three business days to think of the answer?*

Fuck. It was all I could muster in my head. I couldn't speak a single fucking word. I'd just had Mitch between my legs syphoning out *the web of love* from my glory hole. The spicy mayo from not just him, but Roe too. I was a fucking milkshake.

Things were good.

Things were...*different,* having Roe back. It was great for Drip—and me. God, the fucking releases he could get out of me were insane. Not even I could make myself cum like he did. But over the last few months—*weeks even*—it was like Drip had been slowly unloading. He was really something else, and the crown that had been on his head since he started The Underground

147

had swelled. He was becoming his true self. The man I knew was buried there.

Deep in there.

I just needed to see more of it. There was so much more, thanks to Roe.

And there had been way too many times in the last six months that the fucker had near slipped my dirty secret up, giving me a bruise or two that I'd remember. Threatening me that *he* was going to be the one to tell Drip about our *other* brother. He never let the words fall from his lips.

Bluffing.

Always bluffing.

Roe had spent almost every fucking day getting on my nerves, with the same bullshit and the name-calling.

"I know all your secrets."
"You filthy little whore."
"I'm going to tell him everything, and he's going to make you wish you were dead."

Like fucking hell, man. Either grow a pair of balls and do it, or come up with a new threat that might actually scare me. But the truth was, I was scared. I was fucking terrified. Yet I was too stupid to admit that. *Maybe I should come clean?*

I pushed the thought aside. It wasn't the time to be dwindling off with the fairies, which was what I felt like I had been doing the entire time Drip had been gawking at me. He hadn't taken his eyes away from me, not once. He was sweating, drooling, panting and twitching, watching me watch him. And that feeling of him not being able to touch me was beyond anything I could explain. *It hurt.*

I mean...it was no different to any other time he looked at me, especially lately. But this was different. It had been three fucking weeks. Three painful weeks without his touch. And of him giving me the cold shoulder. All because he couldn't be near me without fucking me. And lord only knows if he touched me, he had to fuck me too. He had no control—neither did I. Our lack of control was why I fucked him in the first place. And why I fucked my other brother too, his twin.

Yeah okay, fine...I had the boys to keep my needy kitty company. But they weren't Drip. And it was actually painful, fucking them day in and day out with Drip just sitting in the back watching, waiting. Not being able to have him the way he was dying to have me. Well, that was enough of that.

"Why don't you bring that thing over here and show me then?" I finally muttered out my words...*I think*. Or was I speaking in tongues? I did feel kind of dizzy. Could I handle another round? *Of course I can. I am Twister fucking Rellik. Yes, I chose that last name...fight me.*

If I could handle being fucked into a state of unconsciousness on multiple occasions, beaten senseless by a man who held all my secrets, a bunch of people since I could walk and almost myself, *and* live to tell the tale? Then I could handle a third load of cum inside me. *Especially if it was my brother's load.*

I jolted with a shattered breath fleeing from my lips. In seconds he had banded his hands around my thighs and tugged me down so that the heels of my feet were perched on the lip of my car's bumper. I stopped breathing for a moment, staring into his grey eyes. They were almost black, filled with lust and a terrifying dose of desire, and something else I couldn't quite put my tongue on. My skin felt like it was tearing from the goosebumps. Despite the heat flaring my skin I felt a sensation of coolness overlap me. The anticipation was killing me.

Wait...am I...nervous?

He pressed all his weight on the palm of his hand beside me, flat on the bonnet, and the other over the low of my stomach, right where it felt tender...*and nice.* He leant forward, rolling his tongue over his lips and pushing my belly slightly. My breath started to bounce out of sync, every inhale and exhale rapidly cooling my lips.

Why the fuck am I looking at him like I am seeing him for the first time? I swallowed the knot in my throat, a clear sign that whatever I was feeling was an emotion that I'd not had before.

The chain of his necklace fell forward from the crevice of his neck to his chin. "Drip," I breathed. *Holy fucking hell.*

The jagged edge of his jawline where it began above the tip of his neck tattoo was sending me into a frenzy—it was now fully blacked out. He must have had that done while he'd been ignoring me the last three weeks. The new piece and his protruded adams apple that shadowed underneath were making my heart fucking stop. His deep glare burned between my eyes, then my lips and back again.

Still in time. Neither of us moving.

Breathing.

In that moment, there was no one else in existence. It was just me, and my brother. I shuddered underneath him with need as he pressed down a little firmer.

"You have no fucking idea how painful it is to watch you get railed when I can't even touch you," he purred. The heat of his impatient breath crawling over my skin. I had no words, I just melted under him.

"Drip," I added the single-syllable word again. *Is that really the only thing in my fucking vocabulary?*

"Yes, baby?"

"I—"

"I...I what, sis?" He strung out the words and flexed a brow. *Why am I so intimidated right now?*

"Who are you?" I questioned, certain that I wasn't looking at my brother.

"I am yours. And who are you?"

"Yours?" *Why did that sound like a question?*

"But I haven't made you mine yet. Not until I fill you. That is what you have been wanting isn't it? Me to fill you. Make you mine." He pressed again and the pressure sent a shockwave of pleasure to my spine.

"Ah!" I moaned. *Yes, that's what I want. Give me. Fill me. Claim me. Worship me.*

"Make. Me. Yours." I begged weakly, certain that the words were staggered and laced with a shaky desperation.

"Ask me again," he warned, the colour of his eyes darkened yet the crack of his smile curled on one side.

"Please."

He tilted his hand a little lower, the pad of his thumb just a fraction from the pounding little bud that was waiting for his contact, yet he refused to touch it. *My punishment for not using my words.*

"Make me yours," I said with more haste and need.

"Say my name," he growled. *Jesus fucking christ.* His fucking requests. I was desperate and on death's door, I was certain. My heart was thumping out of my chest.

"Make me yours, *Drip*."

"Can you try the other one?" his voice cracked as his thumb curled slightly so that I could feel the pressure between my slit, but again not touching my needy clit. *What the? He hasn't...I haven't...we haven't. We* don't *say our names.*

"But—"

"I want to try it, please."

The sudden change of his tone was enthralling, and it sent me into a head spin. I was getting whiplash. I hadn't said his name since we first got together, since we fucked for the first time. He freaked out and I didn't see him for weeks. When he came back months later he had new tattoos, and piercings. And said he never wanted to touch me again.

"I can't fuck my own sister. That's fucked up. Look what you've done to me, I'm a mess."

"Please. I'm sorry C—"

"Don't you dare ever call me that again. It's dirty."

The memory of that night seven years ago stung me. I was scared to say his name again. Could I even say his name again?

"Please Bla—"

"Uh! You don't get to say that to me," I hissed, cutting him off. I wasn't *her* anymore.

"Okay. But...I need to hear you say my name, please. For me?" He pressed. His eyes were soft...*desperate*. I was certain I could see his soul. I tried to squirm back slightly to get a better look at him to diagnose what in the ever living fuck was going on inside his head, but he pressed me down even harder than before.

"Cooper?" I squeaked the word. It felt so foreign saying his name again.

"Yes, fuck." He swirled my clit with a groan. Instantly, I felt a weight on my shoulders that had been begging to be released for years finally loosen. I rolled my body back over the bonnet, letting my soul take everything in. "Say it again," he worked my clit as he coaxed the words, sending my orgasm right to the tip of my pussy. My body tightened and tingled.

"Cooper!" I howled his name loudly and shuddered through my climax. "Cooper."

The sensation of darkness closing in from the intense climax, seeing nothing other than stars and shadows. Fluid pulsated from my pussy with each clench from my orgasm.

"Yes, baby, that's right. Fuck."

"Cooper," I repeated again, barely in a breath, barely audible. Then in the midst of total darkness, the pressure of him filled me and my muscles clamped around him. *Like the two of us were made for each other.* He pounded into me with every element of ownership and possession. The head of his cock nudged the forbidden wall, making me gag on impact. I wanted to scream in pleasure and pain, but I was barely able to lift my head. The pressure took my breath away, he was deep.

So fucking deep.

It took everything in me to concentrate on him so that I could savour the moment forever and not black out. When I looked at him again he was in a state of ecstasy—at least, from what I could glance before rolling my eyes back again.

"Oh, FUCK, Twister!" he growled and stilled. An immense amount of heat quickly followed. He filled me with his possessive love like I had been aching for him to do since I first found his camera in my room. The sensation of his climax and ownership riveted through me and formed a concoction with my soul, pulling a tear from my eye. I didn't think he had it in him, let alone his brother.

But one thing I was certain about, was that I belonged to Drip.

Forever.

We are that eternal twisted friction that you spent your entire life looking for.

My addiction.

My elixir.

My king.

And I am his queen.

Ride or die.

TWENTY-ONE
Drip

"ARE YOU READY FOR your first race, pretty boy?" I uttered as I scruffed Mitch's hair up before tenderly locking him into a death grip hug. The heat that was radiating from his body told me that he was probably shitting himself. *The poor fucker, so innocent and sweet.* The chuckle that left my body was almost...*freeing.*

Every*thing* was in the right place.

Every*one* was in the right place.

I was the king of my city. I had my boys, my crew, and *my girl.*

"Can't. Breathe." He tapped at my chest with a cough and I laughed again. Even though he was breathless, he still had a smile on his face. Mitch's pearly white, straight teeth were gleaming from the split of his lips. *So pretty.*

I released him from my hold and gave him a good slap on the ass.

"I'm ready," he finally coughed out between titters.

"How *ready* are you?" I teased again, my tone a little more husky and playful, the twitch in my dick coming to life.

"Umm," he replied with furrowed brows as if he sensed I was up to no good. I winked at him and in an instant his cheeks glowed red. He strummed his fingers through his curly hair, like he always did when he was nervous, and jittered his foot. Mitch's opponent came towards us and I let out a breathy laugh. I tapped over the that was snug in my back pocket and making sure it was still there. *Oh yes, I am up to no good.*

Now that Roe was home, I had a lot more...free time. I had been monitoring Twister's TikTok watch history. It seemed as though she had stumbled across an algorithm of *masked men*. Which made sense, after seeing that porno with the cosplayers that night, her pussy was like a fucking ocean. Night in and night out, I would watch her fuck herself to sleep with either her fingers, her toys or the fuck machine while watching the masked cosplayers. So I figured I'd put the two together.

I want—need—to see how she will react to me in one. I was always trying to fill my sister's needs, and feed her her every desire. No matter the cost.

My little killer.

Butterflies swarmed in my belly, and my dick twitched from the memory of her taking that man's life months ago. *Shit, not now...why am I into that by the way? Why in the actual fuck am I into that?*

157

Because she is.

I shook my head, pulling myself back to the moment and back to the fucker walking towards us that I was now inherently mad at for interrupting my sexual desires. He walked like an idiot, like he had swag. Like he owned the place—or was going to. *Like fuck. No fucking chance, maggot. Keep it cool, Drip...for now.*

"You must be Justin?" I asked the middle-aged blonde with my hand out to his, my tone a little too edgy...and horny. A moment passed and I glared at my empty hand that was hovering mid-air in front of me before pinning my eyes to his. I narrowed them in anger and my lip curled.

Big fucking mistake.

"Yep. So...uh, I was told I get pussy if I win. Where is she then?" His childish arrogant voice curdled my blood, which only made me smile. *Oh this is going to be fucking perfect.* It wouldn't matter if this fuckwit won or not.

He's a dead man.

And didn't that make me full of lustful arousal?

I turned a sideways smile and stepped aside. Twister popped out from behind me at the right time, and as usual, was looking as fine as fuck. She was wearing heeled boots with straps that coiled up her legs that looked oddly familiar. *Are they Ivy's?* And she had paired them with fishnet stockings.

I swear to fucking whatever god exists, those damn denim shorts get shorter and shorter. They were freying and riding up her ass, and if I looked hard enough, I'd see the little heart tattoo on her cheek. She'd had her nails done that morning, sharp black pointed daggers with diamantes on them. *Fuck*. All the better for scratching my back when I cum in her for the umpteenth time.

She stopped before the guy, her arms behind her back with one hand gripping her elbow. *So promiscuous*. She leant in towards him. The fucker was practically salivating at the mouth as he stared at her tits. The little white tee was ripped at the bottom and only just covered her nipples—as per usual—and were pinched rock solid by the way.

I watched in pure suspense, hoping that she would just snap his neck like she did the other guy in the garden. But she didn't...yet. She inhaled his cologne and then circled him, like a fucking predator. As far as hot predator goes, Twister took the fucking cake. The taps of her heels on the concrete echoed through the carport of our meet point.

He swallowed, coughed on his own saliva and then swallowed again as she toyed her fingers at the elastic of his jocks that stuck out above his biker pants.

"Do you want to fuck me?" she led on. Her tone was low and tormentingly dominant, and damn near made me want to beg on my knees and let her have whatever it was she wanted from me. *Fuck.*

"Yeah. I'll take this bitch home any day of the week," he replied, directing it at me, not her—yet without even fucking looking at me. The mere sentence made the hairs on my back stand up.

I wasn't a jealous son of a bitch, but I knew an unworthy piece of fucking shit when I saw one. I was definitely going to enjoy *that* piece of shit. I was certain it was the guy that Roe mentioned seeing out the front of the strip clubs, taking things that weren't his.

"You can—if you win," I conceited. Dare and desire now laced in my eyes, my balls weighing heavily from my arousal. I knew exactly where this was going to go. *Welcome to our hell, Justin.*

"Mmmm, perky tits too. I'd like to shove my cock in that little tight cunt. Have you fucked her?" he deadpanned.

"More times than you've stroked your own cock, my guy," I answered truthfully, with a wink.

"Fuck yeah."

"So here's the deal," I said through a grin as I cracked my neck, swallowing down the daggers. "If you win, I'll let you fuck *my sister.* But if I win, you have to watch me do it."

Silence.

Total fucking silence.

Even though I heard nothing other than the thumps of this guys twitching heart, I just about reckoned I could hear Twister's joy and enthral. Not possible I know, but I suspected it was there. I'd look at her eventually, but I was too busy staring through the glass eyes of this fucker before me—*empty.*

His soul was completely desolated. Only fillable by money, and pussy that he didn't earn. A pathetic lowlife, with nothing to live for. He was absolutely the cunt who walked the allies of the strip clubs for a free fuck. And by free I mean *not consensual.* The anger that raced through my veins was no match for me. There was no way Mitch was taking this guy down in the race.

Sorry, kid. This guy is mine.

It stayed silent for a moment longer before he finally pulled his head out of his ass. "W-what?" he choked on his own words. That was the reaction I was looking for. *The one I always look for.*

"I think you heard me." A pang of desire filled my chest.

"You-you fuck your own sister?"

"More times than you beat your own cock," I repeated the line again. His facial expression was much different than the last.

"Naaa. Fuck that noise. I'm out," Justin responded in disgust, backing away with his hands up. My hard glare didn't let up on him though.

"What? You've lost your taste in my sister all of a sudden, have you?"

Something caught my eye in the distance. *Perfect timing.* Roe was hovering not far from behind Justin, and a piece clutched in his grip, not that the fucker noticed.

"I'm out, bro," he repeated, backing further away, taking yet another step, and another, until he made contact with the gun that collided at the centre of his spine. I chuckled, rolling my tongue over my lips as I walked closer. *Where in the fuck he got a gun from I don't know, but in this precise moment I could not give a rats fucking ass.* What the fuck was I alluding to?

"If you leave now, you're a dead man," I muttered. Well, he was if he stayed too. And I'd make it look like a mistake.

"You're fucked. I'm not doing anything you tell me!" He spat on the ground and I smiled. *Oh, but yes you will.* Stubborn and vexing. Such lies. The piece of shit would do anything for some pussy, even if it meant knowing that it was my sister I was auctioning, off and his death was at the end.

My heart pounded from my chest, and my cock pulsated hard under the fabric that was struggling to hold it down. My nose flared as I stood chest to chest with the fucker. He swallowed loudly as I gestured an airgun to his head, my eyes sparkling in excitement and enthral.

"Say no to fucking my sister again and I'll kill you. I *own* that fucking pussy. So if I tell you to shove that little cock in there, then you'll fucking do it." I roared with very little holding me back from killing him there and then. I had better plans for him.

I *wanted* him to fuck her. I *needed* him to get milliseconds before he came, and then I would splatter his fucking brains to the other side of his skull with whoever's gun was in Roe's hand. And then I'd fuck *his* ass and cum in it, and then let Twister cut his dick off and put it in a jar to keep it as a token.

Preserve it. And maybe fuck her with it. *Yeah, that's what I'd do.*

Oh shit.

Okay, okay. Message received. I was *definitely* into that. It was fucking dark. But no one was leaving that night until the cunt was six feet under.

TWENTY-TWO

Twister

THE ENERGY WAS HAIRY as fuck. I didn't know what the hell was going on, or what would happen. Drip was fucking *ropable*. And it was fucking hot. His flame had no ability to be extinguished. It didn't help that I was the one who was continuing to ignite it.

I knew for certain that Justin—the man that Mitch was *supposed* to be racing—was about to get an introduction to hell. My hell. *Our hell?* What sinistry was Drip unfolding? Was he finally alluding to my darkness? Everything I was seeing in him right then was Cole. *His twin.* That same level of shade that I was drawn to...before he changed.

Before I sent the asshole six feet under. *For abandoning me when I needed him most.*

Maybe Drip had been bottling in all those emotions since. Well, the cap was loose now.

I couldn't help but giggle out loud and clap with glee. My raspy tone only added to the reasons why I was a fucking lunatic. It was fucking electric. *And now there is a gun?* Though a pistol wouldn't be *my* first choice. It never had been...how boring? Where was the fun in that?

"Do you think he could handle a woman like me? With a pussy like mine?" The words rolled off my tongue like I was the one with the pistol and wore a crown on my head. The three of us looked at the guy like we were vultures. My heart picked up the pace, waiting for someone else to say something.

"He's going to find out, isn't he?" Drip's tone married mine, then Roe perked up.

"Fuck yeah, he is."

"Hmm. I like where this is going," I uttered.

I knew what I wanted to do with him the second I saw this guy, feeding off Drip's energy. I guess we were in sync like that. He'd known me since I was little, though I couldn't remember exactly how long ago that was. My life before *them* was kind of a fuzz really. All I remember was feeling cold, sore, and hungry all the time. Seeing nothing other than darkness and then the silhouettes of two boys hovering over me like I was their lost pet.

Their little secret.

Drip had come such a long way. He was such a frigid boy, always under the shadows of his twin. Who was my favourite

165

of the siblings...*as kids*. Cole was like me—the outcast. Falling into my darkness and encouraging it, becoming it. *Until high school*. He was too perfect. He wanted the blue-collar life, always wanting to change me to someone that I wasn't.

You couldn't change me. I wasn't normal.

I remember always pulling the wings off flies, and spitting blood from my steaks into a glass...*and then drinking it.* I was drinking tequila before class and snorting coke at lunch. Selling cigarettes to minors. Having sex with anyone I could sponge money from. But after all that, how was I the one to get suspended if I was the one getting raped by my fucking teacher?

Karma had come back around quickly though. *Don't fuck with the bitch that had access to needles and peroxide.* Apparently, being a violated rape victim as a minor wasn't a good enough excuse for killing a man for my own safety. A month in juvie for me and a slap on the wrist for him. With my history, no one ever believed me. Not after those articles about me. Except for Drip—after he found me on the bathroom floor that night.

Cole was the one who wanted to change me.

Cole was the one who got in the way of everything.

Cole was the one who called me a daddy killer and a mummy murderer...like those articles did. Yet he didn't oblige to being in my pussy.

"You will always be unwanted."
"Even your own blood didn't want you."

"Who would want to call you Mum?"
"Your kid will just be as fucked up as you.
You're ruining our lives. Our family's name."
"Do us all a favour and die. Take your disgusting unborn child
with you."
"I don't want it, or you."

I felt heavy in my chest as Cole's words from nearly eight years ago burned their way into my heart. I quickly swiped the tear that threatened to fall from my eyelid, swallowed the knot in my throat and grabbed the flask from my glove box.

With shaky hands and an emotion that I hadn't felt in years, I slugged down several, excessive gulps of the Bacardi, letting it burn my throat. Extinguishing whatever feeling that was in the pit of my stomach. I sat half in and half out of my car, waiting for everyone else to turn up. I made sure I had gotten there first, have a fucking minute to myself. Though there was a crowd behind me, they meant nothing to me.

I could hear the roar of bikes echoing in the distance. It was Mitch, with Ivy as a backpack. Good, the others wouldn't be far off. The night's race was by far one of the best routes The Underground ran. They would head south-east through the tunnel under the city and then through Zig Zag. Tight corners, steep accents and *complete darkness*. It was terryfing even during the day, but at night—pure adrealine.

"All good?" I asked them, as wired as I was earlier.

"Mhmm." Ivy nodded, deciding to stay sitting on the bike.

"Uh, I think so. Can I have some of that?" Mitch asked.

"Have at it." I gestured as Mitch took a swig from my flask, before walking back to the bike and passing it to the blonde. I liked her. Whenever she was around, Roe was slightly more docile...*slightly*. She was a good fit for The Underground, as was Mitch. They just all seemed to gel. *Probably because they are so obedient.*

Ten or so minutes had passed and there was still no sight of them. I scanned the horizon and Mitch stood beside me, playfully tapping his hip into mine as if we were best buds—with benefits.

"Where are they, do you think?" he asked, his tone somehow soothing the worry that laced my chest. *He should be here by now.* From where we were standing, looking down over the city—Drip's city—you could see everything. It was beautiful from up there. I searched every corner and every drop.

"Did you think Justin was going to go easily?" I said bluntly.

"True. True," he added, choosing to stay silent for the rest of the time. *Finally.* Flickers of lights paced through trees, but were gone faster than I had the ability to locate them. I held my breath, listening to my surroundings. The engine of the bike Drip swapped with Mitch sounded through the trees. The 1,300CC motor becoming clearer as it narrowed the distance, powering Drip through to the finish line.

He was the first to speed over the crest of the hill, faster than I had ever seen him race. Justin followed shortly after as he rolled over the apex, with Roe behind him and a gun hooked in his left hand.

"Hah, the dick head," I muttered under a breath. *Maybe he tried to run off, what a fucking loser—weak.*

Mmm, I like what I see. I trailed my eyes over Drip. He had parked barely three feet beside me, his corded muscles reacting as he revved his bike. That damn singlet was so tight. Drip had beads of sweat pooled over his body, and his chest was racing up and down. My heart raced faster and faster as he took his helmet off. It was like falling in love with him all over again, but in an entirely different way. I knew for sure he was feeling what I was feeling.

He was fizzed, riled up. Whatever static energy that was bouncing off him had a direct path to my pussy. *Fuck, now I am really horny.* And there was that *itch* again. That scratch that I never seem to have the ability to lul. Like last time in the garden, but it was much stronger than the last.

I wondered for a second what my car would look like with thick, crimson liquid over it...and my cum, and Drip's. Blood and cum.

Yeah, that. That is what I want. I was certain that Drip wanted that too.

So fucking twisted.

Drip threw his hands around me, and in seconds his lips were sealed over mine, his fingers digging into the firm flesh of my ass. His tongue dove into my mouth with such need and hunger, as if he was claiming me there and then, confirming my every thought. *He is going to be the homicidal one tonight.*

"Mmm," I groaned into his mouth as his warm metal bar swirled around my tongue.

I could even taste his rage. It was fucking delicious. It was making me ache, everywhere. *Is this really going to happen?* He broke contact with me, leaving me breathless for only a moment to catch myself again.

"Can you do something for me, baby?" Drip asked with a layer of need. Though it wasn't a question—it was a demand—one I'd only be happy to obey.

His steel eyes were cold, yet full of entice. Staring into my very soul with every ounce of dare, and desperation they could regulate. All I could do was stare into them and lose myself there. *All these years, would you not understand that I would do anything for you? Anything? You don't need my permission. Just tell me. Okay, now say that. Why won't the words come out?*

"Anything," I breathed the only word I could put together.

"I want you to kill him," he whispered and then paused, scanning my face for answers. I couldn't help but feel dejected. I didn't want to kill him—I wanted *us* to take his life—together.

His lips opened again to speak, stretching into a grin and his eyes smiled with him before the words followed. "With me."

My heart skipped a beat and for a second, I thought I lost all control of my legs. "Do you think you can do that for me, sis?" he added. A moan slipped my lips and I connected with his again. His fingers curled into my skin deeper as he groaned, our darkened desires entwining together like cracks of lightning.

"Yes. Yes—God, fucking hell yes," I hissed. *This is finally going to happen—together.*

"Fuck. You're so good to me." Drip praised.

"Your twisted little secret?"

"My twisted. Little. *Killer.*" He growled between kisses, referring to my last name. Which was ironically spelled killer backwards. *Clever me.*

Fuck.

TWENTY-THREE
Drip

WHEN YOU THINK THE adrenaline couldn't rush through your veins any more, Twister showed you that it could. The hooks, turns, ups and downs of Zig Zag were no match to the energy of *her*. Not even the drop offs that were narrow as fuck with *no* barriers. Not even at night time—one small mistake would cost you your life.

Two hours. Two hours was all it took to make my point. *I will always fucking win.* It was *my* fucking city. *My* fucking girl. And that fucker was about to take his last breath.

I groaned once more and my eyes narrowed with a famish I could no longer control. The woman had my heart and soul in the palm of her hand, everything in my body straining for her needy breath under my skin. Just when I thought I had the power to release her from my hold and begin our next task—*to kill*—I squeezed her ass again and lifted her. She gripped me tight with her legs around me and drove her kiss into my chest.

She drew her hands from the arc of my neck to my cheeks, the soft pads of her thumbs toying with the sharp edges of my facial features, only fueling my need for her. I moaned as she tilted her hips forward and back, grinding on the swell of my cock that ached and throbbed for her.

"Baby, are you ready?" I whispered, regretfully needing to break the seal of our bond before I fucked her there and then. There was time for that, but we had other things to do.

"You have *no* idea." Her soft needy tone in the heat of her exhale tore down my spine. I fanned my eyes between her hazel ones once more, seeing that glint that had been there since the day we met. *She was born a killer. Who am I to stop her from staying one?*

I lowered her to the ground and she twirled on her heels, swaying her hips with each step back to her car in that way. *She knows exactly what she is doing.* I turned my attention to Justin, who was still pinned by Roe, with his arms behind his back...and gawking at my sister *like she was his dinner.* He strained against Roe's grip slightly, but it wasn't as if he was screaming for his life. Not yet anyway.

As far as he was concerned, he just thought he was going to get a free porno and be the star of the show. Because that *was* the rule—become Twister's fuck toy. But what he didn't know was the blood shed that was about to unfold between my sister and I.

Twister sat on her bonnet with a joint in her mouth and her legs out, one crossed over the other, hiding that perfect little pussy, waiting—*to kill for me.* She loved being the centre of attention, all eyes on her, never doing anything fast. It was always slow and sensual.

She blew the cloud of smoke from her nose and pushed her chest out, enough to see her tight midsection compress, the strokes of her muscles pulling, and the shadows of the lighting working everyone's cock—and Ivy's pussy so it seemed. *God damn.*

"You see, Justin...look at that pretty little thing. You know what happens now, don't you?" I stepped closer to him, pointing at her and glaring right through his eyes before grabbing his chin between my thumb and index finger. "Don't you?" I repeated, my tone husky and strung out.

He didn't reply straight away, but then Roe knocked the back of his head forward with his palm. "Ahh—Jesus fucking christ. Yes, okay. You're going to have sex with...*your sister.* You freaks," Justin snapped.

"Yes. Good boy. And you're going to watch." I smirked.

"I thought part of this whole thing was that I could fuck her, even if I lost the race? But she's your sister, man. What type of club are you running?" Justin's face scrunched together in disgust, but yet again not entirely objecting to the idea.

"*My club?* Are you really questioning *my* club? Right now?"

"No." His throat struggled against his swallow.

"Then you would do well to stay quiet. Oh, and don't worry, we're still going to be nice. We will let you cum, won't we guys?" I paused to look at my crew before hounding my glare into his eyes. "That's going to be the best part," I said truthfully—just to him. He scoffed under his breath, locking his chin nervously.

"Never. Wouldn't even get hard, mate."

Twister laughed. "It wasn't an option," she added, blowing another cloud into the air.

"What about us? Do we get to?" Mitch's voice sounded, I had almost forgotten he was there. *Yes, you too, but the bloodshed is between me and Twister.* My cock twitched. *Come on, keep it together.*

"Could this loser handle watching *all* of us?" I spoke loudly so that all could hear, even the mob in the distance who was watching on. Justin's cheeks flushed crimson, his body straining yet again against Roe's firm hold, but he wasn't letting him out of his sight. The menacing energy had ricocheted like a domino effect. What started off with just me wanting to bury the cunt six feet under, was now five.

"I have a better idea," Twister called over me. "If he's going to refuse to fuck me, and thinks he can manage to watch everyone else fuck me *without* getting an erection so easily, then he can go."

"Okay, deal. What do you think?" I asked Justin.

"Easy. And I can take my bike?"

"Sure," I smirked.

Twister took another long drag of the weed-filled doobie and passed it to Mitch, who had moved to stand next to her car with his arms crossed. We all watched, completely mesmerised as she shuffled off her car and stood before Justin.

She flared her lashes up and down him. The man was already melting like butter—nothing unusual for Twister. His palms twitched behind Roe, and he looked as though he was restraining everything in him to stop himself from touching her. She didn't move. She just stared right through him. Who would break contact first?

Moments passed and she was still holding her breath, ironically doubling the effect of the Marijiana. I watched eagerly as the speed of his chest rising and falling became faster by the second.

"Getting nervous, are we?" Roe asked him, his ashy tone was edged with darkness and delight, but Justin didn't reply. The heat in my veins escalated as she leant in, inches from his lips, on the tippiest of her toes before letting out the entire chestful of haze in his face. Without delay she rolled the flat of her tongue along the base of his collarbone, trailing up to his stubbled chin. But again, he did not move or whimper.

"Kiss me," she lured him through her promiscuous voice and body language. Roe chuckled under his breath, though it was no humorous laugh of his. It was almost...condemning.

"That's not fair," Justin croaked.

Twister's teeth peered through her lips in that seductive grin, and then he took his lips to hers. She let him devour her for a moment before leaning back and turning the palm of her hand over his chest, pushing him slightly.

"No—not there." Her tone was soft and in full control. He dropped his gaze to her chest and Roe released his grip. Justin slowly bent down, lifting her tee above her breast and mouthing her nipple with his tongue. She dipped her head back with a loud moan as he played with her piercing, before finishing it off with a giggle.

"No. Not there either," I added for her.

I walked over to them, stopping before Twister and slowly unbuttoned her denim shorts. I tugged them down over her waist and they fell to the bitumen around her ankles. She breathed heavily and turned her knee outward so that more of her was exposed.

"So needy. My needy little minx." I barely formed the sentence. I went for her G-string and rolled my index finger under the fabric, pushing through her wet slit. *Fucking hell, I am so fucking horny.* The sound she made before swallowing enticed the groan to form deep within me.

"So fucking wet for Justin, aren't you? Or is that for all of *us*?" I stopped for a second to pull myself together. "Kiss here," I ordered.

"Fuck," Justin breathed.

"Yes. We will." Twister just had to add to that. But I knew that tone. All lies. All bluff. All play. *That's my girl.* Get him up only to bring him back down again. He mirrored the sound she made, totally spellbound by her. I didn't know a single soul on this earth who had denied her and lasted another five minutes before succumbing to her siren.

He got to his knees, taking his hands to her ass and spreading her pussy with his thumbs. I licked her flavour off my finger, tasting her sweet desire with a hint of bitterness. She pushed his head into her and he sealed his mouth over the heaven of honey, nodding his head three times like he was bopping for apples before she pulled him back by the hair to look up at her.

"You want me?" she teased, egging him on. Justin was speechless for a second, but nodded his head vigorously.

"Yes, yes, yes. Yes, I—please. Please." He swallowed and went to go back to her pussy, but her grip stopped him.

"Then get in line." Her tone was blunt and cold. *Minx.*

She stepped out of his grip, pulling her shorts back up and buttoning them again and strolled back towards her car. Roe grabbed Justin's arms before stringing them behind his back once more without so much as a struggle or objection.

Twister glanced back over her shoulder at the five of us who were all practically drooling by this point—even Ivy. She tilted forwards and my cock pulsated as her taut jeans rolled back down over her toned ass. Music wasn't playing—not even a hum of a car or bike—but the song 'Porn Star Dancing' by *My Darkest Days* started running in my head. Because my filthy little sister had begun fucking strip teasing as if we were in a fucking strip club.

"*Shit.*" Roe, Justin, Mitch, Ivy and I said the word in unison.

TWENTY-FOUR
Twister

IF YOU HAD TOLD me when I took the life of my first victim, that I would be here where I was, about to fuck four guys, a woman, *and* kill a guy—again. I'd have laughed in your face.

I had everyone in a frenzy. I started slowly reaching down around my ankles, showing them just how flexible I was. I swayed my hips and then unhooked the straps of my heels before tugging down all the little strands that coiled around my leg. *Thank you, Ivy, for letting me have your stilettos.*

"Holy fucking shit. Who is this girl?" Justin whimpered.

"Mhmm. I know." Drip replied.

I smiled from my efforts. They were getting hot and flustered. I leant on the bonnet of my car and peered over my shoulder again. Waiting. *Who will be first?*

"Mitch? You're up, pretty boy. Bon Appetit," Drip commanded. Mitch placed himself behind me, already eager to take me. He planted the flat of his hand over my ass and slid under the straps of my G-string, pulling it down and letting them fall around my ankles.

In one swift movement, his jeans were down and he placed himself into me. I winced as his thickness filled me, taking my breath away. No matter how many times Mitch and I had sex, I always struggled to accommodate him. He was just one that I could never truly adjust to. He bent his arm around my hip and reached to find my clit.

"You feel so good tonight," Mitch moaned in my ear as he rubbed my throbbing little knot, pushing me very close to a climax.

"Oh God." I tightened around him as the pleasure intensified. His fingers circled a little faster, then slower, and then faster. He had gotten awfully good at doing that. Goosebumps rose over my skin and I suddenly became aware of the sensation of liquid dripping onto the low of my back. I shuddered. Ivy had moved beside us and was trickling water over me.

"You ahh, looked a little warm there. Does this help?" she flirted. Having her next to me made my stomach swirl. *This really is my favourite thing—fucking in front of people.*

"Yes. But now you're making me hotter. So I guess that means you're next then," I teased. She smiled nervously and then nodded. Mitch licked up the water as he pleased my clit and pushed me over the edge. I clenched tightly and unfolded into my climax, unaware that I was crying out for Drip.

"Fuck. Fuck. Fuck," Mitch groaned, grabbing my hips to pull me into him harder, riding through my pulses and then filling me with his hot thread. He panted and tucked himself away, then stroked my ass softly. "You okay?" he whispered softly so that only I could hear.

I nodded mindlessly, and he took the bottle of water from Ivy and dropped to his knee. He took a mouthful of water and inspected my pussy with his fingers, gently caressing the area, which felt...soothing? I let out a breathy moan as he slid his tongue into the hole that he just claimed, and filled, pushing a mouthful of water into me before sucking it back out—and swallowing. *He is too good to me.*

Every emotion that raced through my veins was heightened. But the one that was impossible to ignore, was *the itch*. To scratch to taste just a touch of the other guy's blood.

To feel a kill again.

"Atta boy." Drip praised as Mitch wiped his mouth with the side of his arm and walked back to them.

"Take your cock out. I want to see how long you last," Drip spoke from the side of his mouth, directing the comment to Justin.

"Really?" Justin stuttered under his breath but Drip didn't answer.

I turned to face them and pulled myself backwards up onto the bonnet like I had done earlier and spread my legs. I flicked my long, sweaty hair off of my shoulders and it floated over my back. I playfully swayed my legs open and closed again—teasing, panting and hungry. Seduction and mayhem was written all over my face. *Fuck. I am incredibly horny.*

I looked at Justin, seeing that he was covering his dick with one hand, the other behind his back, where Roe still held him tightly. Roe's facial expression hadn't changed a great deal, but his eyes were darker and filled with hatefuck—that look only I knew and loved. *God, he hates me so much.* And at that moment, that only excited me. I knew he was just dying to put me in the ground for what I did to him, but fucking me unconscious was the only way he could get as close to my death as possible.

"Take your hand off," Drip demanded. Justin did, revealing for certain that he did in fact have an erection. A pathetic erection. *I think my pinky finger is bigger than that fucking thing.*

I directed a wink at Drip and his jaw bulged with tension. I could tell he was on the edge of snapping. Impatiently waiting for his turn. I craned my neck, finding my petite little blonde toy and gesturing my head for her to come closer.

"Come on," I called.

She stood between my ankles, her eyes politely trying to stay on mine but involuntary dropping between my thighs. Her panting grew faster as she narrowed her gaze on my pussy, and then a frown surfaced on her face.

"I didn't realise you had a tattoo there," she squeaked. Her voice edged with nerves and excitement as she visually inspected Drip's name on my pubic area—the closest she had gotten to me since the night we first met. Every other time she had just been either in the same room with me or in the garden. I smiled because it was me that was going to fuck her, not my brother, not Roe, and not Mitch.

"Why don't you touch it?" My flirt coaxed her to my body, luring her to touch me. I hadn't been with a woman since I was...maybe nineteen. My feelings towards her were very different to the last. I mean, I had mentally threatened that if she laid a hand on my brother I would chop her clit off. *But that thought is neither here nor there.* She planted her finger on my skin and traced over the letters down my pubic area. I moaned from her soft touch, making my heart race. I had forgotten how good a female's touch was.

I glanced over at Drip, who was smiling proudly, and then I thoughtlessly lost myself in the memory of waking up to a new tattoo—and a really soaked pussy. He had filmed the whole thing for me—one of my favourites to playback. I was unconscious and had no recollection of the whole tattoo, so watching it made me feel as though I had been mentally there. He had dragged out each stroke of the letters between pushing his cock into me and pulling out again. Pushing in, fanning another stroke to the letter and pulling out. Pushing in, another letter, pulling out again. Drip more than fulfilled my fantasy of somnophilia, it was diabolically the best fucking experience that I'd asked him to do. *The things this man will do for me.*

"Did this hurt?" Ivy asked, her finger right on the top of my clit, pulling me back to reality. *My piercing.*

"You talk too much. Now...fuck me," I ordered, almost a warning. She followed my direction quickly, adjusting herself so that she could insert her fingers into me. Despite Mitch's best efforts to clean me of his cum with water, my body had made another round of secretion and was yet again wetter than the ocean—no H2O to pussy juice malfunction. I could hear the soft little whimpers of the others bouncing through the air as they watched her push past the swelling of my pussy. They sounded closer, but I ignored them—losing myself in pleasure. She knew *exactly* what she was doing.

I rolled my hips to meet both of her fingers as they curled firmly against the roof of my pussy, allowing her to put more pressure against the tender area under my pubic bone. I shuddered.

"More. Yes!" I shrieked a moan as she gestured the *come here* motion inside me, tampering with the knot that was my g-spot. I heard another desperate groan from beside me and followed where the sound was coming from, seeing that Roe had shoved Justin right beside me.

Pre-cum.

Dripping in waves over my bonnet from Justin's cock. "I knew it," I chortled the words before inhaling a rough breath. The thought of his blood all over me and my car only enticed me to get him to reach his climax sooner, and I was nearing mine again.

Fuck, I love this.

I need this.

Always.

My nipples pinched hard with arousal until they were sore, and my skin burned like it was about to ignite into flames, my chest dried and refusing air. With every orgasm Ivy gave me with Justin beside me watching and pulsating, I grew darker and darker. Building the need for his blood. I held onto my every need and whim to push through until I didn't think I could last any more.

I still had Roe to go before Justin touched me.

"Roe? I need you, please."

TWENTY-FIVE
Drip

ROE FUCKED MY SISTER like it was the last thing he would do in his life. Like it was the last thing *she* would ever do. Pumping into her harder and harder with each thrust, making each of her wails of pleasure and pain ricochet through the curves of the road we had raced up what felt like hours ago.

I glanced quickly at the time on my phone with my free hand, my other one fisting Justin's shirt. Not that the fucker was going anywhere. He had been mesmerised by her since she kissed him.

3.27 A.M.

Fuck. We'd been at it for nearly four hours and the cunt was no closer to death than he was four hours ago. Twister was wasting away to a puddle of cum and sweat before me, and I had no idea much much longer I could deal with seeing her that way. But she was holding out. *Just for me. Just for us.*

"Alright, big boy. It's his turn now."

Roe growled nothings under his breath but retreated from Twister hesitantly and took my place holding Justin, deciding to keep himself out of his pants and continue working himself. *God damn.* It pulsated hard for him, coated in Twister's gloss. Justin's face looked pale and totally disgusted by what Roe was doing behind him.

What we are doing.

To my sister.

But did he really have a choice? *No.* Not that it stopped the pre-cum from flowing from him. He had been edging himself the entire time, sweat pouring from him to the point of him almost in tears for not being able to relieve himself—which he was *dying* to do. I was convinced he was foaming in the mouth for it—for her.

I pushed Justin between her legs and grabbed the mask from my pocket then threw it over my head, leaving it above my nose. I mouthed, *"its go time"* to her and dropped the balaclava over the rest of my face. Her face lit up and her eyes twinkled in pure excitement, seeing me in the mask. Justin acted quick, bending his knees to place his very eager—*and very small*—cock into her with an immediate groan and a shudder. Without him noticing, I pulled the knife from my other pocket that I had taken from Roe earlier and gently placed it in Twister's hand. The sound that she made when she grabbed it was orgasmic.

"Good girl, take him. Tell me, sis, how does he make you feel?" I asked, my voice muffled from the mask. *Come on, baby, you can do it. Make him bleed. I want to see you covered in red.*

I stepped aside and groaned as I pulled my cock's foreskin back, rolling it down and back up again. My balls tightened from the pleasure of finally touching myself, after watching her for so long.

"Oh, I'm feeling something," she snarked sarcastically as he put all of his effort into fucking her.

"Yeah, take my big cock, slut," he cooed. He almost softened my cock in an instant. *Pathetic cunt. Not an inch of pleasure on her face and yet he is still going at her like she is enjoying it. What a deadbeat.*

Twister wrapped her legs around him, strategically locking him into place as she moaned occasionally for theatrics. She rolled her eyes as she shifted the knife just up above Justin's waist and then hovered there. *Fuck, fuck this is happening.* I rocked my hips gently, taking short and quick breaths to my strokes. I needed to slow down. I eased my hand and waited, watching, panting. *Needing.* It was so fucking wrong. But it was everything she had been wanting, I fucking knew it. I'd only be more than happy to give it to her. Always.

A laugh slipped from her lips as she trailed the jagged edge of the knife up his back. Twice, three times, four times—like it was nothing.

Blood.

So much blood.

Twister was moaning and shuddering as he bellowed in pain and squirmed, which made Roe laugh, loudly.

"God damm," he said.

"Don't you dare fucking move!" Twister hissed at Justin, the knife pushed firmly on the pumping artery on his neck.

"Fuck," I added. The red trail of his blood started flowing down his ribs onto the car, pre-cum coated my hand and my arousal flooded my brain.

Using the knife, she forced him over and onto his back. Justin whimpered but followed her direction, crying like the little bitch he was. She mounted him and guided his still-hard shaft into her before running the knife down his neck as she grinded him. She trailed the weapon under his shirt and the fabric split in two, showing more of the crimson liquid.

Twister rode him, hard, rolling her hips and using her fingers to make herself cum—twice. Justin was fading in and out, yet maintained his erection somehow. His face was fucking terrified, whitening with each slash she tore over him.

His blood had more than smeared all over the bonnet. It was seeping into the engine bay and dripping onto the road. But still, it wasn't enough. I wanted *more*.

"More, Twister. Come on, baby. Show me what you can do," I coaxed her as I sped up the grip on my dick. She snickered through her panting and bounced on the tip of his pathetic little cock. He whimpered and tensed.

"Oh, FUCK! I'm-I'm cum—!" Justin's vein from his face protruded as he began to climax. But Twister showed him no mercy. As he cried out in pleasure, he also bellowed out from the wounds she pressed into him. As she dug into him, she kept rolling her hips, cumming again, and again, and again, until there was no colour left on either of them other than fucking red. *Oh, sis. She is spent.*

"Such a good fucking girl," I groaned my praise for her under the fabric. She followed my voice, tipping her head around to meet me and then holding her dripping crimson hand out for mine. Exhausted and bathed in blood, cum, sweat, and dare I say it—satisfaction.

Not yet, sis. He's not quite done yet, I said in my head as he coughed, choking on his own blood. She muttered my name—my real name—twice. Like music to my fucking ears.

"Tell me you need me. I want to hear you beg for your brother," I demanded as I stripped off the rest of my clothes, letting them fall to the ground and leaving my mask on.

"I want you. I need you, please," she begged. I took the knife from her other hand and then turned her over so that her back was flat on Justin's body. Without a moment to spare, I pushed myself into her and we both slid upward from my strength. Everything was completely covered in the thick

191

residue of Justin's blood, his soft, fading gargles he was letting out only enhancing the moment.

Twister moaned and clenched tightly around me. Considering how exhausted she was, she kept herself ready and needy for me.

"Ah. Fucking hell, Twister," I hissed through grit teeth as she climaxed for me. I brought my forehead to hers, losing myself entirely in her eyes as she looked into mine through the mask. I glided my now-scarlet hand down her cheek, trailing red lines over her skin. I pushed them into her mouth, and she mounted in a way that I had never heard before, sending me into my own orgasm. "Yes. Fuck. Yes," I moaned loudly, hearing the echo of my growl ricocheting through Zig Zag. *This.*

This was what we had been looking for.

This was...*us.*

I pulled off the mask and caught my breath. A moment or two passed—or ten or twenty—and I whispered between each kiss on her lips, tasting the metallic flavour of Justin.

My.

Twisted.

Fucking.

Sister.

I shifted myself off her, admiring the carnage that was before me.

"See Justin? I told you. I told you you had to watch me do it," I said roguely to the lifeless carcass under my sister.

TWENTY-SIX
Twister

WATER. HOT, STEAMY, WATER. How many showers? How many showers did it take to scrub off the stained blood of a dead man that was lodged in every nook and cranny my body had?

The answer was one, but it lasted over an hour.

A whole day *and* a whole night after I had done the thing—*murder*—with my brother.

I scrubbed my wet hair repeatedly with the towel in the mirror, not really noticing the reflection. The woman standing beside a smear of Justin's blood in the mirror smiled at me, her eyes holding a familiar cold and black glint behind them. I drew my hand to my raised cheek that was pulled tight in a grin, like the Cheshire cat. Confirming that what I was feeling was what I was seeing. That woman was in fact *me*.

I was more *me* than I ever had been. More myself than ever. For the first time in my fucking life, I felt like I belonged. I finally belonged within my actual self.

It was the real me.

Unhidden.

I was radiant. *A radiant killer?*

"Twister Rellik," I muttered to myself. *Twisted Killer.* The name I had made for myself all those years ago.

I knew who I was the second I took the lives of my parents. They were never the same after what I had done to my sister. I mean...I only wanted my parents to myself, was that so hard to ask for? They didn't have time for me any more—they didn't love me any more. *What is it about younger siblings?*

They take everything away from me.

The memory of my childhood struck my mind like it was yesterday. My parents had found me in my room covered in blood...with my sister's head in my lap, and her body on the floor. After that, I knew for certain my parents didn't love me. They tried getting rid of me by any means possible. Beating me into the ground never worked—it was just fuel to my fire. Bleach though...well, that fucked me up, and nearly killed me. Fried my insides, and my brain. So I killed them too—which wasn't easy by the way. You'd be surprised how much of that stuff you need to flood the veins of a 120-kilogram man.

I had no one. And then the twins found me...the fucking twins. *Do you know how hard it was to separate them? That was my hardest secret to keep—loving one more than the other.* They both loved me more than anyone ever had. I felt normal again.

They didn't think I was weird. They didn't want me dead. *Until one of them did,* and then he stopped loving me...and his unborn child.

A tear threatened to leave my eye, but I flicked it away before it had the chance and threw my towel on the floor. I walked out of the ensuite to my wardrobe, pushing aside the knot in my chest. I jolted, not expecting to see Roe on my bed.

"Fuck—you dick. You scared me."

"What are you doing in my house? Come to rescue this old damsel for her birthday?"

"Nope." His eyes wandered my body. *Here we go again...another threat up his sleeve, no doubt.* The broken record was getting old. He sat there with his arms crossed, staring, not doing a damn fucking thing.

"Take a picture, why don't you? It'll last longer," I snarled and pressed my tits together with my tongue out.

"Okay." He shrugged and pulled his phone out for a quick snap. I tuttered with an eye roll before continuing to my clothes. "Do you feel better now?" His voice pitched up a notch to reach me across the other side of the room.

"You mean, do I feel better after killing someone...again?" I asked.

"Yeah."

"Yeah," I mimicked him, adding a little sass to my tone. I walked back out, throwing what I collected from my wardrobe onto the bed and pulling out a G-string from my bedside drawer. I put it on and turned my attention to a crumpling sound, like paper unfolding from a scrunched ball. Roe was unfolding something in his hand. I knew exactly what it was—how in the fuck did he find it?

That fucking article.

"How many's that now—" Roe snarled, anger lacing in his tone and his eyes suddenly pure black, which shifted to look right past me before he continued. "—*Blaire*?" he added bluntly. My heart fell to my stomach. *I don't think he's messing around this time.*

And if the timing couldn't have been any fucking worse, who was the silhouette to fill the door behind me? Drip.

Fuck. How long had he been there?

"What do you mean, how many?" he asked nervously.

"Wait!" I wailed, quickly throwing the shirt over my head.

"The name, Phantom...really lived up to his name didn't he?" Roe teased. I swallowed hard, snatching the article from his hand. Shredding it in my hands and dwindled to the floor.

"What does he mean, Twister?" Drip demanded. My stomach was in knots, and my throat was not swallowing the ball of tension.

"Roe," I objected, shaking my head.

"Oh, but yes. He deserves to know doesn't he?"

"Please."

"I deserve to know what? Twister?" Drip's face was pale and low. It was almost like he had already worked it out...but didn't want to accept.

"Tell him or I will," Roe threatened immensely, my face was now pure fucking terror. I couldn't tell him. *I can't.*

I won't.

He will never love me again.

He's mine. I'm his. It was supposed to be just us forever.

"I-I-I..." I stuttered. A single tear pooled at the base of my eye and fell down my cheek, and then another. Which Drip only copied.

"Deserve to know what?" he pressed, the tone of his voice already heaving with hatred for me. My heart pounded like it was about to climb up out of my chest. *This is it. This is the end of us.* Just as we began.

I closed my eyes and sighed. *One. Two. Three.* Only the sound of my heartbeat thumping in my skull told me that I was still alive. A moment of self solitude passed and something inside me suddenly switched. Darkness. Emptiness. Isolation. I opened my eyes, looking at Drip, then Roe.

"Fine. Have it your way."

Without even hesitating, I stepped closer, feeling the heat of fear that was radiating from Drip, then parted my lips, curling them slightly. All emotion fled out the door. I looked right down the barrel of my brother's soul, who was on the brinks of tears.

"I. Killed. Cole."

I swallowed the lump that had swelled in my throat and took one step back, and another, and then bolted. Leaving every memory, every emotion, every kiss, every smell, every "*I love you*" behind.

I *never* looked back.

TWENTY SEVEN

Drip

Three years later...

I SAT SILENTLY ON MY motorbike for the evening, my legs perched over the handlebars and leaning backward with my arms behind my head. My view was nothing but spectacular.

For the third year in a row, I overlooked the city that was once mine as the sun collapsed behind it. Not all that far from the place I never thought would be the last place I'd see *her*.

I hadn't been back there since then. *I couldn't.* Everything reminded me of her. Every*one* reminded me of her.

For the third year in a row—to the day—I'd lost myself in every sacred moment I had with her. The woman I called my sister. My heart ached for home...*her*. But she was gone. And yet the memories weren't, as much as I tried to forget. They stayed with me, even after I had burned everything after she left.

Everything.

It was her birthday, or what *we* called her birthday. The day we found her. And it was the hardest day within the other three hundred and sixty four days of hell that I had to push myself through.

"Happy birthday, T—Blaire," I mumbled under my breath as I looked at one of the shooting stars above the city. Three years later, and my hell hadn't gotten any easier. Would it? Probably not. I could deal with losing my brother, my twin. But losing Blaire was the hardest fucking thing in my life.

I closed my eyes for a moment, listening to the silence of the road when my phone buzzed. *Weird, no one has this number?*

Unknown number: I miss you

My heart sank. Even without any context, I knew it was her. I left the message on read, deciding to put my phone back in my jacket and not reply. I hated her. *If you did, you would have deleted the message.*

"Fuck," I sighed. Seconds passed and it buzzed again. I flicked my screen alive.

> **Unknown number:** I know you're ignoring me

I hovered my thumb over the keys for a moment, then tapped my reply. Slowly.

> **Me:** What do you want Blaire?

The three dots appeared quickly and then the message filled my screen. My heart rate was intensifying for some reason.

> **Unknown number:** Blaire now? Jeez, that cold? I haven't been that bitch since we were kids

I didn't reply straight away. I knew she was playing games with me, and I wasn't fucking having it. *Did I really mean so little to her?* All I wanted since the day she left was for her to apologise. And maybe we could have moved on. But she left me when I needed her most. She left me when she needed me the most.

> **Me:** You are Blaire. Nothing more, and nothing less

I licked my lips, wiping away the salty tear that had buried itself there. I sighed deeply and hit send. It was a complete fucking lie. She was, and always would be, Twister. She wasn't Blaire. Not really.

> **Unknown number:** So bitter. And on my birthday?

> **Unknown number:** Hey, fun fact…sometimes I thought of him when I fucked you, but then I remembered…he was dead. And his baby too. And then I was stuck with his weak twin instead

Whiplash.

That was what I fucking had. A full whirlwind of *what-the-fuck.*? I considered throwing away my phone and never owning one again, but I didn't.

His baby?

Is that what all this was about? It didn't make any sense. I drew my palm over my head and rubbed it, looking for an answer I didn't have. *The night I found her in the bathroom, with the bleach and... the coathanger...that was that?* My stomach flipped. *Doesn't she know that I was the one who was always there for her?* Me. Not Cole. Not her parents. Not mine. *Me.*

> **Me:** Why are you doing this?

I hit send, not knowing what else to say to her. Everything hurt. Everything ached. All I wanted was to hold her and tell her that I loved her. Make her believe me. Inject the words into her brain. *I fucking love you.* Nothing could come between us—not even what she had done. I wanted to tell her that I would have never abandoned her. I couldn't hate her for what she did, I tried to, but I could never.

If only she could see that.

> **Unknown number:** Because I hate you

> **Drip:** Oh yeah? Well guess what? Sometimes, I hate you!

> **Unknown number:** Then come and fuck me like you hate me… big brother

I waited. Waited for the words to come to me.

Do I burn my phone and forget this ever happened?

Or do I bite into this, and ignite the friction once more?

Rule my city again.

Bigger.

Better.

With my little minx. My ride or die.

My twisted, little sister.

Twister.

Me: Meet me at the finish line?

My reply was left on read for what felt like an eternity. I was becoming more restless by the second waiting for her to say something back, but she didn't.

"What if I win?" Twister's voice spoke from somewhere nearby, startling me. It took me a damn hot fucking minute to reboot, pull myself together and find another string of words to say to her after fumbling about and *not* falling off my bike.

Given how much she liked to delete people from existence, the sultry look she had in her eyes could mean one of three things. She wanted to *kill* me, she wanted to *fuck* me. Or *both*. But even then, seeing her standing before me with her hair in a messy bun, a tight pair of black leathers and her helmet resting on the side of her hip, there was also another look about her. Behind the sass, behind the sultry, behind the lust...was guilt.

I knew she didn't want me to fuck her like I hated her, even though I absolutely would. That was her way of self punishment for what she had done. Twister was the worst for self sabotaging. But I figured I'd let her roll the dice, playing along with her little game until I was blue in the face. *Or try to anyway.* Maybe then she would realise that I would rather die than to leave her.

"Well, then," I said as I hopped off my bike and walked towards her. "I guess that makes *me* the plaything doesn't it?"

By the time the last word had left my mouth my body was up against hers and my hands were behind her neck, forcing her gaze upon mine. My soul ached for hers as I gripped her tightly. A warm gasp flew past her lips, and her body released whatever tension she had built up, her weight softening under my touch.

I trailed my thumb over her bottom lip and drove my hungry grey stare from her eyes down to her perfect peachy mouth, and back up again. It was like seeing her for the first time—instantly two souls falling in love and needing one another. I repeated the pattern until she swallowed tightly. Inching closer and closer so that my breath was so close, it was almost hers.

Her lips tremmered under my thumb, begging for me to kiss her, but her words failing to exit. So I whispered.

"I *could* be your plaything. I'd never turn down the opportunity to be at your feet. But," I paused to loop my finger through the hair tie that held her bun loosely, pulling until her long tresses fell around her face before continuing, "my darling minx. My little sis. What makes you think that you'll win...*this time*?"

The End...

If you liked this story, please consider leaving a nice review on my Goodreads and Amazon.

If you really really liked this story, and you'd like to read it as full siblings instead of foster, it is available as an ebook or signed paperback on my website.

www.laylamoonauthor.com

ACKNOWLEDGEMENTS

Hello, my darkling. Firstly, I'd like to thank you, *the reader*. You've come along with me on this wild journey, finding yourself now smack bang in the middle of my chaos. Some of you came from my debut novel, some have only just found me. Either way, I am forever grateful for allowing me to fuck with your mind, *just a little*. I see you, I want you to know how much you mean to me. Every like, every comment, every single word. I see you. I hear you. I feel you. I love you!

I'd love to thank my imperfectly perfect morally grey husband, who is part PA, part author, part plot thinker, part entertainer, part dad, part mum, part single wife, part chef, part cleaner, part grocery shopper, part chauffer, part plans man and event organiser so that I can learn to drift like Twister, *dramatic inhale here* and everything else in between so that I can continue to do what I do—**write.** I couldn't do what I do without you, baby. It simply just wouldn't happen. You make me a better writer. You make me a better mother. You make me a better wife. I fucking love you!

My beta readers, Jade, Denise, Justine, Aidan, Makayla, Abigail, Tylisha, Jess and Maxine. You have allowed me to harass you on short notice because I had written a whole ass book in five weeks and needed your eyes where mine failed me. I appreciate every single one of you, and I hope you realise you're stuck with me for life now, right?

My deities, Jade, Maxine, Jess, Lea and Eunice. You have all been with me from the very first video I posted on TikTok in 2023 about my new debut novel that I was writing, and stuck like glue since. For believing in me when sometimes I think I don't have what it takes. For holding my head up when the haters and cancel culture tried to kill me from the inside out and pushed me to where I am today.

My PA, Jasmine. Ma'am, you saved my bacon on more than one occasion. You just whipped up everything and took the jobs I had piled up, and took them on like they were nothing. I value you so much and I look forward to growing with you as a team.

My editor, Brittany. BRITTANY!! FUCKING BRITTANY! Where have you been hiding? I wish I found you when I first started this career. You are a fucking Godsend! I truly mean it. And I am certain on many occasions I had you questioning your career choice with me, and your endless supply of messages, sweaty face emoji's and GIFs was evidence of that. I wish I lived closer so I could drop off some towels, we all know you needed them. I'm proud to call you my editor, from here on out. I won't hesitate to kidnap you either, you're *mine,* bitch.

Lastly, I'd like to thank myself. Like I always do, and will never stop doing. For learning to grow, develop, change and master this life of writing. For accepting that this career has its ups and downs, its good and ugly, its hard and easy, its victory and defeat. And for *always* finding strength to come out on top of it all.

With all that said, I have two tattoos on my leg which I would like to read to you. And I want you to take them with you in your brain, wherever you are.

"She wears strength and weakness equally well. She has always been half goddess half hell"

"Just like the moon, she must go through stages of emptiness to feel full again"

ABOUT THE AUTHOR

Layla Moon is an Australian writer, she lives in Perth with her morally grey husband and three children. Plus the four legged children also.

Her favourite thing in the entire world, (on days that aren't her husband) is music, wine, coffee, and biscuits.

Apart from having a sick obsession with metal music, she likes to write and entertain the minds of many. She has a heavy sense of humour, has no filter and yet is somehow very bubbly. Above all else, in this journey...

She has found her true self.

Because it's only when you risk failure, that you discover things.

And she can't wait to discover more in this path she calls 'writing'.

If you would like to stalk me, all of my information is on the next page

STALK ME

TikTok

Instagram

LinkTree

Made in United States
Troutdale, OR
12/04/2024

25923042R00133